Through the Eyes of the Orcas

My thanks go to:

Alexandra Morton. Her book "Listening to Whales" was my ultimate inspiration to write a story from the orcas' point of view.

The scientists Dr. Paul Spong and his wife Helena Symonds (Hanson Island/Canada), for their long-lasting research work on the communication of the orcas, for their informative homepage, for providing the OrcaLive-Community, where whale fans from all over the world have the daily opportunity to put up-to-date news and links online and where the orcas' calls are broadcast live (see appendix), and last but not least for the fantastic foreword which they have kindly provided for my story.

U'mista Cultural Society in Alert Bay/Canada for their magnanimous permission to use the Indian legend by Henry and Helen Hunt.

Jan van Twillert. He gave me a lot of helpful information and corrected the orca family tree. His homepage (see appendix) was indispensable.

My husband, Dr. Hubertus Thomas, who contributed a lot of good ideas and who offered constructive criticism bravely, even though he was well aware of my potential reactions. ☺

Christine Sawinski, for her tireless proofreading and her honest opinions on my manuscript and the great translation.

Ilka Sampel and Leona Niedzwiedz for their help with the correction and Leona for the fantastic photo of an orca which I was allowed to use, not to forget her many heartening e-mails.

Friederike Braun, because she devoted her time to this story.

All those who encourage me in my work.

My further thanks go to: Julia Neider (WDC-Germany), various visitors to the OrcaLive Community, my daughter, who made up the names of the two main characters and my son, whose eye adorns the back of the cover.

Homepage: **www.doris-t.de**

Through the Eyes of the Orcas

Translated from German into English
by
Christine Sawinski
(except original source of foreword and legend)

Imprint
second edition © 2017
© Doris Thomas, Pfaffenhofen an der Ilm/Germany, 2010
Original title: „Mit den Augen der Orcas", 2009
Illustrations and text
Photo of wild orcas with kind permission by Leona Niedzwiedz
All logos in the appendix by courtesy
Production and publishers/Herstellung und Verlag: BoD – Books on
Demand, Norderstedt, D
ISBN: 9783-746016597

Contents

Foreword

Even for those who love Nature, there seems too often a barrier that keeps us from fully understanding nature's wild characters. Only through our imagination, can we travel to the other side.

Doris Thomas, through her charming story, Through the Eyes of the Orcas, gives us this rare chance to experience, for a time, the world of the orca. Personally, after many years of learning about orcas, their amazing behaviours and wonderful sounds and cultures, we are also acutely aware that the actions of humans have created dangerously precarious conditions, throughout the world's oceans, for all who live within.

Whales, both large and small, are still hunted, their food is disappearing from over fishing and habitat degradation at alarming rates, their world is being poisoned from man-made toxins, the ocean is inundated with industrial noise, and global warming is intensifying the pace of decline. The scariest part of this reality is that all this has happened within just a few lifetimes, before we have any chance to fully explore, experience and understand the ocean realm.

Ms Thomas' book is very timely for it generates and fosters a vital empathy and caring for this alien but wonderful world beyond the edge of land.

By Helena Symonds & Paul Spong
May 2008
Written as a foreword for
Through the Eyes of the Orcas by Doris Thomas

If I...

Dolphin! If I could see with your eyes,
what would I discover?
Grey is your world, colours are alien to you.
Perhaps thus you see things
as they really are.
Would I perceive reality?

Dolphin! If I could hear with your ears,
what would I discern?
Silence is unknown to the sea.
Sounds are everywhere, even coming from you.
The echo shapes an image.
Would I listen to the truth?

Dolphin! If I could talk with your voice,
what would I say?
Each sound has a function.
A multitude of information.
Vital!
Would I be able to lie?

Dolphin! If I could swim with you,
what would I experience?
Weightless. Boundless.
Without home.
Without the burden of possessions.
Would I find the meaning of life?

Map of Vancouver Island

Habitat of the Northern Resident Orcas

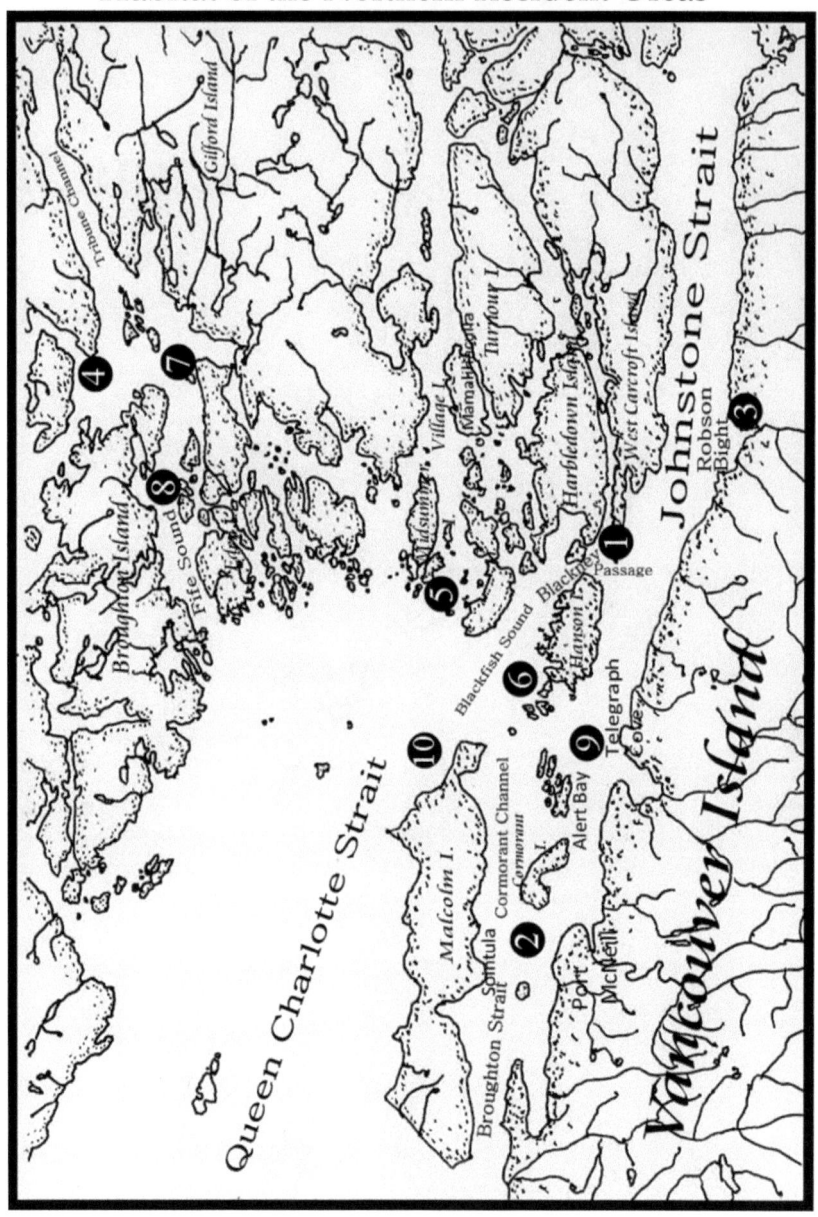

Key to the Map

Key to detailed map

1 Blackney Passage (Time of Remembrance)
2 Region of Silence
3 Robson Bight (Rubbing Beach)
4 Test of Courage
5 The great Gathering
6 Lesja
7 The Tareefans
8 Savage Hunt
9 Whale-Watch
10 Dolphins

Orca Family Tree

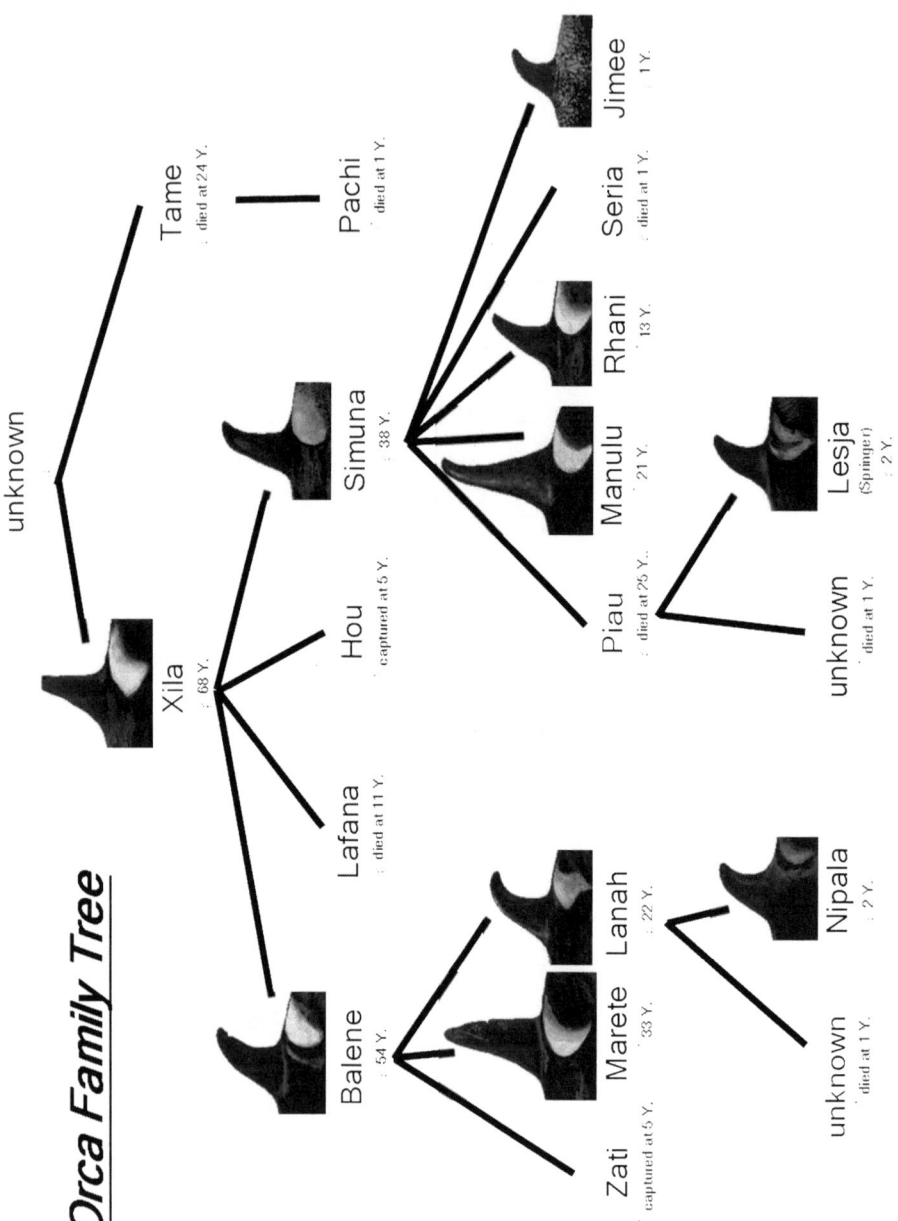

Prologue

(After a legend of the <u>Walas of the Mamalilikala</u> *clan, a tribe of the Kwakwaka'wakw Indians, by Henry and Helen Hunt, courtesy of U'mista Cultural Society.)*

A long time ago, there were some young boys practicing shooting with their bows and arrows. They were paddling in small dugout canoes, out in front of their village called 'Mimkwamlis, known as Village Island. Then, they saw at the point, a pod of killer whales playfully swimming by. The whales were surfacing and spraying water from their blowholes.

The young boys looked at the killer whales and started to discuss shooting at the whales to test their shooting abilities. The boys decided the dorsal fin would be the target and this is what they would aim for. One of the boys shot his bow and arrow and hit his mark, wounding one of the whales.

This made the whale very sad. Then, the family of whales became very angry and swam towards the children. The young boys began to paddle quickly in their small canoes and were dragging them up the beach as fast as they could. One of the killer whales caught up and was right behind the boy who had shot the whale. When he reached the beach he tried to jump off the canoe and run up the beach. As he landed on shore so did the whale. At that moment the whale's dorsal fin turned into a man and caught the boy. The man grabbed him by his Achilles tendons and said to the boy,

"As long as you live, you will never be able to walk properly and you will always suffer in pain, from the muscle in your heels being pulled out, for I am the Killer Whale".

From that day forward the boy and his people respected the killer whales because they were human also, and had the spiritual power to transform. The boy's clan named 'Walas' then took the crest of the killer whale and painted it on their house fronts, they also composed songs and dances to honor the whale. Still today, the killer whale is respected and regarded as being the same spirit as man.

(English original)

Killer Whales

End of school. "At last!" Lisa sighed, "I thought today would never end." She swung her heavy schoolbag over her shoulder. Peter also grabbed his backpack. "You're right, but there is still such a lot of work to do. Old Wittberg condemned us to do this presentation, remember? Can you tell me why you volunteered for THIS topic of all things?"

Lisa grinned. "Killer whales? Doesn't it sound cool? What's the problem? I thought things couldn't get bloody enough for you. *Killer* sounds really promising. Hopefully this means that I don't have to do all the work as per usual with our presentations." Peter answered this snide remark with an unmistakeable grunt. Lisa patted his shoulder and laughed: "It's ok. So far we've always managed. And with this crappy weather we have nothing better to do, anyway."

Together they headed for home. Lisa opened her umbrella and Peter pulled the hood of his jacket over his head. The two children attended Junior High School. They lived next door to each other and spent a lot of time together. Whereas their classmates had started avoiding the other sex, this had not occurred to Lisa and Peter. Perhaps this was due to the fact that Peter had never cared particularly about being "cool" and Lisa was not "ladylike".

Together they walked to school and back every day, helped each other with their homework and studied for exams. When two pupils got an assignation it was understood that they would do it together. Once again Lisa had volunteered to do the presentation with Peter, even though she was well aware that he liked to shirk his responsibilities and that she would be preparing the major part of the presentation on her own. But they always had a lot of fun and usually Peter came up with a lot of amazing ideas. This really made up for his laziness.

"I'll be at your house around three", Peter said when they had almost reached home. "Ok, but please dig out everything you can find about killer whales. And..." she raised her arms as for a quick prayer. "...don't forget to bring the stuff along when you come over!"

Peter rolled his eyes. But he knew that Lisa's reproof was not entirely unwarranted. It would not be the first time for him to turn up on Lisa's doorstep empty-handed. When his friend disappeared behind her front door, he had to smile as he walked on. He was sure that Lisa would provide a load of books and Internet printouts later on, so why exert himself?

Three o'clock in the afternoon. Lisa looked at her watch. When had Peter ever been on time? She sorted out the books on animals and laid out her Internet printouts carefully. It was amazing what she had been able to find on the various web pages of the societies and organisations. The information about appearance and size of the whales tended to repeat itself, but sometimes she came across some facts that seemed unusual. She would go through the lot with Peter.

She had chosen four marker pens in different colours so that they could start right away. Ten minutes later the doorbell rang and Lisa's mother opened the door for Peter. "What kind of weather is this you're bringing along, Peter?" she asked jokingly and Peter peeled off his wet jacket. "It's raining like mad! Darn, now the poster is wet!" He shook the raindrops off the paper and wiped it with the sleeve of his sweatshirt.

With the wrinkled poster under his arm he listlessly climbed the stairs leading to the first floor. Lisa was waiting for him with a grin on her face:

"Oh, you did actually bring something. Surprise, surprise!" Triumphantly Peter raised the poster and waved it around. "I'm marvellous, right?" he stated proudly. "You're a genius!" Lisa stated and took the poster. "Looks like your booty got a nasty bashing. You didn't think of using a plastic bag, by any chance?"

Peter pretended to be offended and shrugged his shoulders. When he saw that Lisa had found a place to hang up the poster he grabbed the sellotape and handed her four strips.

16

"I don't know what you want; it still looks quite good, doesn't it?"
"Well, so-so. In any case we can't show it at school anymore." The paper had become quite wavy with the raindrops and the poster was no longer even. The killer whale, which was swimming towards the beholder under water, had become slightly blurred and its contours grew hazy with the up-and-down of the paper.

While Lisa was still checking whether the poster was straight, Peter approached her desk and noticed the pile of information material. "Are you crazy?" he snorted, "You don't seriously want to read through all this, do you?" Lisa darted an angry glance at him. Instead of answering she pressed half of the printouts into one of his hands and a green marker pen into the other.

"Get a move on!" she snarled at Peter. He sank onto her couch wearily. He quickly checked the number of sheets in his hand and groaned. Lisa grimaced. Then she sat down on her desk chair with a jerk, grabbed the second half of the printouts and started marking individual text passages.

Peter capitulated.

Lisa wouldn't relent. This was very obvious from her pinched expression. He accepted his fate and studied the information he was holding in his hand. After reading a few lines he dared to raise his head and glance at Lisa. She cleared her throat pointedly and continued reading. Obviously there was no escape for him.

After a few more lines he raised his head again and gazed out of the window. The rain was pattering against the pane and it felt like it was night already, because it was so dark outside. The water was hitting the roof above their heads. Because of the sloping ceiling the room felt more like a shelter than a room in a house. The rain was pattering onto the tiles and the water was rushing down the slant of the roof above them. The gutter ran directly underneath the big, sloping roof window. The water was burbling into the drain incessantly and, following the slant, pouring down towards the right edge of Lisa's outside wall, where it disappeared into the downspout in a wild eddy. A continuous swooshing and gurgling could be heard.

Lisa did not appear to be bothered by all this noise at all.

Fully concentrated she was studying page by page, occasionally using the marker to highlight certain text passages. Peter was dozing while Lisa kept reading diligently.

"Did you know that killer whales can become up to almost ten metres long? Amazing!"

Peter lifted his head wearily. "Oh, yes, quite big, those beasts." Lisa shook her head uncomprehendingly. "You do know that they are not fish, don't you?" she asked mockingly.

"Of course I know that. They are mammals. They breathe through lungs and therefore must surface regularly. They have warm blood, approximately 37° C like us. They bear living sweet little babies and suckle them with milk … blah blah blah."

"You see", Lisa hissed, "so much for sweet little babies. It says here that a newborn killer whale is up to 2.50 metres long. So much for being little. And they weigh around 180 kilograms already. Just imagine! I weigh only 41 kilos." Peter nodded appreciatively: "Wow, you're right, that is awesome. The poor mother whale." He screwed up his face, as if twisted with pain, and made a sound of exertion. "Press! Press! Press!" Lisa rolled her eyes. "Boys!"

Once again she became engrossed in her papers. Even Peter glanced at the pile of information, hoping to find some unusual facts. "Oh no", he exclaimed suddenly, "Forget about the killer whales. They are really called orcas or sword whales (*in German: Schwertwale*)." "Well", countered Lisa, "here it says that they are also referred to as *killer whales*, because they sometimes feed on other mammals. For a long time they were even considered to be dangerous man-eaters."

"And do they really eat us?"

"It doesn't look like it. There isn't a single proven case where an orca has attacked a human being. At least not in the wild. But there were a few incidents with animals in captivity, some of them even with a lethal ending. But it is a fact that there is a subgroup of orcas who actually attack dolphins, seals, sea lions and even large whales.

18

They are called *transients*, which means roaming whales. Apparently they are really vicious. Disgusting!"

Peter's eyes widened: "Really? Sounds exciting. Do you have any pictures?"

He jumped to his feet, hurried towards Lisa's desk and grabbed the books. Lisa gaped at him. She would not have thought Peter capable of such enthusiasm. Peter found a photo in the third book, in which an orca was hurling a seal into the air. Full of triumph he presented the photo to his friend. "But most of the killer - er - sword whales feed on fish. Salmon, as far as I know", Lisa remarked on glancing at the photo in disgust. "Why are they actually called *sword whales?*" Peter asked himself and went back to the couch. He remembered a text passage, which he had marked previously. When he had found it he read out loud: "The sword whales get their name from their giant, sword-like dorsal fin, which can become up to two metres high among male animals."

He got up, raised his hand and tried to indicate a height of two metres. Both children turned their eyes to the poster on the wall "Wow!" they exclaimed in unison.

The lights flickered for a moment, while lightning flashed brightly and shortly afterwards thunder crashed outside. "Hey, that was close", Peter remarked, while Lisa moved her swivel chair away from the window surreptitiously. Of course she did not want to admit that she found heavy thunderstorms somewhat eerie. To be afraid of thunderstorms was typical for girls and therefore completely uncool.

They both went back to their papers. Somehow a competition had started about who would be next in finding some interesting facts.

Suddenly Peter jumped to his feet again. He planted himself in front of the poster and pointed at the open mouth of the whale. "Just look at those teeth. Any idea, how long they are?" Lisa shook her head. "Each one is about 7.6 centimetres long with a diameter of 2.5 centimetres. Whales have 10 to 14 teeth on each side of their jaws, that is - er..." "40 to 56 teeth altogether", Lisa interrupted. "Exactly", Peter agreed, "that's an awesome set of choppers."

There was a vivid flash of lightning, immediately followed by rumbling thunder.

Lisa tried to concentrate on her papers once more. "There are orcas who live in close family units. That sounds quite congenial. They are talking about an area near Vancouver Island in Canada here. Some scientists have been conducting research on orcas there for the last 30 years. Dr. Paul Spong and his wife Helena Symonds live there in the OrcaLab, their research station on Hanson Island, and listen to the whales via loudspeakers around the clock. They also note all reports about sightings. They research the orcas, which are called the *Northern Residents. Northern*, because they live between the northern half of Vancouver Island and the mainland. *Resident*, because they are more or less settled there. Look, here's a map."

She showed Peter the piece of paper. "Well, alright." Peter replied slightly bored. "They have counted 233 orcas there. They know each individual animal and for some of the whales they know the complete story of their lives. Cool!"

"Don't you have anything more exciting?" Peter asked. Lisa studied the map, then continued reading. "Here's something you will like. A lot of the orcas die during the first year of their life. I am sure they are eaten by sharks. What do you think? It seems that it hits mostly the firstborn." Peter shrugged his shoulders. "Perhaps they are too stupid to look after their offspring."

"Possibly. It says here that the year before last another one-year-old animal disappeared, a female. But something else must have happened here. The mother was never seen again, either. It was her second offspring, anyway, not her firstborn. Wait, here is something else. The young one was initially seen with another group in the same area. Strangely, at the beginning of this year it was found with the *Southern Residents* all of a sudden. As a rule the *Southern Residents* and the *Northern Residents* don't even meet. The scientists were able to identify the young orca without any doubt. The little one seems to utter a special sound, a call which had also been heard from her

20

mother. That's what is says here, anyway. Also she has a light patch behind her dorsal fin ... wait ...", Lisa went through the pile of papers on her desk, "... the patch is called saddle. In this patch there is a very distinctive dark colouring shaped like a C, similar to a slender crescent. They call the young female SPRINGER."

"And what's so exciting about all this?" Peters screwed up his mouth.

"Just wait! They want to try and return the young one to its family in the north. There are a lot of islands in this area." Lisa once more showed the map to Peter. "Springer doesn't seem to be able to find the way back on her own. It is a miracle to the scientists, anyway, how the little one has survived without her mother so far. Now they are planning to bring her back to her family to increase her chances of survival for the winter."

"How are they going to do it? They can't possibly put such a big whale into a bag and carry it – hey presto – somewhere else", Peter asked incredulously. Lisa continued reading: "It doesn't say. I am sure they will have a plan. Here's something else: Cool, the scientists have placed microphones in the water in the area around the research lab on Hanson Island and even transmit the sounds live on the Internet."

Another flash of lightning illuminated the room, followed by booming thunder. The sudden illumination created capricious patterns on the wavy poster. For a split second the whale seemed to be moving.

Involuntarily Peter shrank back. Lisa also seemed to have noticed the uncanny change in the poster. "I found a CD with whale songs in my brother's room", she said without averting her gaze from the poster. Peter stared at the whale on the wall: "Put it on!"

Lisa turned around and switched on the CD-player. Then she got up and joined Peter. Gradually the orcas' sounds could be heard. Softly at first: "Eeeoooooo." The pitter-patter of the rain was still louder than the recording. They were both intrigued and watched the orca in the poster.

21

"Eeeooooooo!" The volume of the recording increased. Gradually the voice of the whale dominated the noise of the thunderstorm.

"Eeeooooooo!" It made Lisa's flesh crawl. Peter grabbed the fabric of his jeans with his fingers.

"Eeeoooooo!"

There was an enormous crash as lightning struck nearby. It was more than one flash of lightning. The first flash blinded the children. They closed their eyes reflexively. With the second and third flash Peter and Lisa stared at the poster in confusion. And they were sure that the whale had moved. They opened their eyes wide.

Was the whale moving towards them? Was it possible? There was another flash of lightning and they were able to distinguish a definite movement.

But this was impossible!

The next flash of lightning was so bright that they once again had to close their eyes. The mighty thunder startled them. All of a sudden there was a power cut. For a moment it was completely dark.

Absolute blackness made their surroundings disappear. Time seemed to stand still. Lisa and Peter held their breath.

"Eeeoooooo!"

Peter

Lisa

"Lisa, where are you?" Silence. "I feel funny. Lisa?" No answer. "Lisa?"

"Peter? What happened? I can't see anything."

Lisa's voice reassured Peter slightly. "Nor can I. I feel as if I am floating. I can't feel the ground beneath my feet." "Nor do I. Can you see anything?"

"No."

They were surrounded by darkness.

Both Lisa and Peter held their breath. Seconds passed, then minutes. Surprisingly they both did not feel the need to fill their lungs with air. They were underwater.

"Eeeoooooo!"

Like a sword cutting through a black cloth with its sharp blade, the sound tore the darkness. A grey wall of slick shimmering stripes appeared around them. It turned out to be long plants of seaweed. Slowly the plants were separated and a mighty shape made its way through. At first it was blurred but then the picture became clearer.

It was a killer whale. "Eeeoooooo!"

"They have arrived! Listen, everybody: They have arrived!" Lisa and Peter perceived a voice. There was no doubt. The whale who was swimming towards them had just spoken. Shortly afterwards they could both feel a tingling feeling on their bodies. *Drrrrdrrrrrdrrrrrrdrrrrrr.* What was that?

Utter confusion followed next. Full of panic Peter turned around towards Lisa or rather towards the place where Lisa's voice had come from. But where was Lisa? An enormous orca was swimming next to him and eyeing him.

"Liiiisaaa!" yelled Peter frantically. "Peeeeteeer!" shouted Lisa, equally horrified. They both pivoted around and scanned their

24

surroundings for the familiar sight of their friend. They called incessantly.

"Where are you? Peeeteeer!"

"Liiisaaa!"

But all they could see were two orcas. They both knew that the orca in front of them … yes … this orca had somehow come towards them out of the poster. But where did the second orca come from? Peter saw it on his right side where Lisa should have been. Lisa, however, discovered the orca on her left, where her friend Peter had been a minute ago. But where was Lisa? Where was Peter?

"Peter?" Peter kept staring at the whale next to him. "Lisa?" Lisa looked deeply into one eye of the orca next to her. She could not see both eyes at the same time, as the second one was on the other side of the head. "Is it you? Peter?" "Lisa? Lisa, is it you?"

Two orcas remained quietly side by side. Then they turned around slightly and started sending out exploratory echo clicks towards each other. *Drrrrrdrrrrdrrrr drrrrrdrrrrdrrrr*

"Lisa"

"Peter"

All had changed.

"It is time to surface", the orca prompted them. All of a sudden the children became aware of the need to breathe. Without thinking they moved to the water surface and exhaled, even before their blowholes had left the water. Shortly afterwards they inhaled the fresh sea air deeply and felt an enormous energy inside themselves. It was completely different to breathing as a human. Not such a matter of course and incidental, not controlled by reflex. As a human one never thought about breathing, one just did it. Now it was different. They exhaled and inhaled consciously. They decided when the time had come to fill their lungs with oxygen. And they filled them more effectively than they had done as humans. As soon as a human exhales the urge to inhale follows immediately.

This had changed. They were able to control their breathing. Within minutes Peter and Lisa had understood, how their oxygen supply had changed.

All had changed.

Surprisingly the children had no problems at all coming to grips with their new bodies. They did not miss their legs, they just used their mighty flukes. The flukes were moved up and down with strong muscles. With their pectoral fins they were able to steer in any desired direction. It was child's play.

Like astronauts in space with zero gravity they floated through the water and manoeuvred their torpedo like bodies without any apparent effort. There was nothing to suggest that they now had a weight of almost three tons each.

All had changed.

At seven degrees Celsius the water was much too icy for humans. But now a layer of 15 centimetres of fat protected their bodies from hypothermia. This so-called blubber prevented their body temperature from dropping below 37 degrees. But the first barrier against the cold water was their skin, which had an astounding thickness of two centimetres.

All had changed.

The children had changed into orcas. Not only did they look totally different, their senses also functioned differently. Their sense of hearing was much better and they were able to detect even the faintest sound. This was not surprising as not only their way of hearing had changed but also the medium in which they now lived.

Water transmits sounds five times better than air. Their lower jaws now picked up the sound waves, increased them and transmitted them to the tiny ears, which were hidden underneath small skin folds on the side of the head. The range of sounds, which they were now able to create, had also increased enormously. They managed very low sounds, which could not be achieved with human vocal

26

chords. They equally succeeded in creating high, shrill calls, which would have driven away the entire audience of an opera performance.

They no longer created sounds with vocal chords but with air-filled little sacks below their blowholes. Through sudden contractions of these sacks the air was squeezed in and out, thus creating a sound. This sound then radiated into their foreheads, where it was amplified through a special mass called melon and released into the water. Echo clicks constituted a particular mode of orientation, where sounds in short succession were reverberated from all kinds of objects. Such a sound lasted no longer than a hundredth of a second, not discernable individually by humans. The whales received the echo and were able to detect distance and nature of the object through the slight discrepancy between the original sound and the sound of the echo. The whales were able to apply this special skill, which is for instance shared by bats, within a radius of 1,500 metres. They only sent out the next click after the echo had come back. This means that the intervals between the clicks depended upon the distance to the object, which was scanned. To humans this echolocation sounded like *drrrrdrrrrdrrrr*.

All had changed.

Even though they now "saw" the world with their ears, their eyes were still in perfect working order, with one vital limitation. The eyes of a whale lack the ability to see colours. They were now able to distinguish between countless shades of grey but they no longer saw the beauty of colours. Everything was black and white. They were colour-blind like all whales. Apart from this limitation they were able to see above water just as well as they had been used to as humans. Below the surface, where the human eye has great difficulties with its contact with the water, a special layer of skin protected their whales' eyes. Not only that, they were able to adjust their eyes with muscle power. Thus the picture was also crystal clear under water.

27

Seawater filters the light. From a depth of three metres onward red disappears, at five – six metres orange, shortly afterwards yellow and at a depth of 23-27 metres finally the colours green and blue. After that the world appears to be grey only. As this is the depth where the orcas mainly stay, this is probably the reason why they lost the ability of seeing colours during the course of evolution. They had no advantage from this ability, therefore it was redundant.

But the environment was full of fascinating colours. Above water there were islands with green forests and rocky shores in various stone colours. The sky was shining with an intense blue and under water multi-coloured fish were swimming through seaweed, which was gleaming in dozens of green hues. But for Lisa and Peter the world was grey from now on.

All had changed.

 **The Guest Family**

"Everything ok?" the whale next to them asked. The last few minutes had passed so quickly but seemed to have lasted almost an eternity.

They were now whales, orcas ... killer whales.

"I'm fine", Peter remarked and Lisa agreed with him: "I'm alright, too! But this is a bit crazy, isn't it?" Peter had to laugh: "No kidding."

They circled each other. "Cripes, you look strong!" Peter eyed Lisa. Her dorsal fin curved backwards evenly. Her saddle was white and looked almost like a minimized mirror image of her fin. Lisa's eyespot was rather pointed at the end of her head.

"Wow!" Lisa noticed her friend's distinctive dorsal fin and the noticeably curved saddleback. The underside of Peter's fluke was a shimmering white. He was slightly bigger and stronger than Lisa. This is usual for toothed whales. In this aspect they resemble the human race, the males are usually bigger than the females. For baleen whales the opposite is true. The female animals are larger than the males.

The "new" whales circled each other again and again and marvelled at their counterpart. It was foreign and still somehow familiar. The feelings of the humans in the shape of orcas were spinning over.

Finally the orca, who was obviously much younger, addressed them again: "If everything is ok with you I will tell the others that you have arrived. By the way, my name is Jimee."

Jimee turned around and swam off. Without moving Peter and Lisa were able to follow her with the help of their new skills, at least acoustically. They sent their echo clicks after her and they learnt that more orcas were nearby. Because they had such sharp ears they could even understand what Jimee told the other whales: "Our visitors have arrived. There are two of them. I told you I would be the first to see them."

There were nine whales altogether at some distance. After Jimee had delivered her message, the group started moving immediately. They were bearing down on Lisa and Peter. *Drrrrrrdrrrrrrrrrrrr.* The children's skin tingled. But they also sent out clicks towards the approaching whales and thus they were able to "see" the whales before their eyes could make them out. They were impressed. They should really have been afraid but the whales radiated a familiarity, which Peter and Lisa could not explain. They were friends.

The formation of the ten orcas was impressive to look at. The leader of the group was the oldest female, Xila. She was already 68 years old and, following the old traditions, the head of the family, the matriarch. Her daughters, Balene and Simuna, were swimming directly behind Xila. Balene was accompanied by her giant son Marete and her daughter Lanah. Lanah's two-year-old little daughter Nipala did not leave her side. Simuna also had offspring who followed her closely: Manulu, a grown-up male, Rhani, at 13 more or less a teenager and her youngest daughter Jimee, who still depended on her mother's milk.

Lisa and Peter were fascinated. They had not uttered a single word during the last few minutes. They were both far too preoccupied with their new impressions. It was not easy to understand what had happened. Nothing was as it had been before. They were living in a different element, water. Their bodies had changed significantly and they possessed skills, which were very different to those of a human.

The orcas approached the children in total accordance. They each seemed to occupy their special place in the group. The family appeared to be relaxed and in total harmony. Lisa and Peter waited for them to arrive. Even though they were not afraid, they were very curious to learn what would happen next. They were now whales. They were both fully aware of this fact. But they still had a human mind. But did the approaching orcas know who they were, or rather WHAT they were?

30

"Welcome", Xila called from afar, "welcome!" Her voice sounded old and rough, and her skin did no longer gleam like that of the other whales. An exuberant *Hello* from the other members of the family followed. They all introduced themselves and gave their names. The children marvelled at the various orca bodies and tried to remember as many distinctive features as possible.

The female whales had a curved dorsal fin, mostly only half the size of the male version. From the side they looked like a wave surging over a groundswell, obviously about to break. Only Xila's dorsal fin lacked this backward curve and the tip of her fin was missing altogether. This shape looked unnatural as if it had been cut off. Balene had a small groove at the back of her fin. Marete and Manulu, the adult males, had giant dorsal fins. Marete's fin was broad and looked like a sail. Above water the back edge flapped slightly to and fro. It also showed a groove.

At 21 Manulu was twelve years younger than his cousin. His dorsal fin was also giant but much firmer and had a slight curve towards the tip. Rhani's fin still looked very similar to that of a female. He was only 13 and would have a growth spurt this year. Nipala and Jimee still had very small dorsal fins due to their young age. Jimee's body was covered in white spots, which set her apart from all the other orcas

These were the first impressions, which Peter and Lisa had of their guest family. But they realized immediately that they would not be the last. These were not just any orcas, who welcomed them. These were not just orcas, reduced to their black-and white colouring and the shape of their bodies. Each of them possessed not only a number of distinctive body features but also his own character. Each of them had his own personality.

31

 **First Experiences**

The orca family admitted Peter and Lisa as a matter of course. They were visitors, but they were not just tolerated but accepted by the family as full members. The children had to learn a lot to be able to survive with their new bodies in this world that was so different to their own. The family seemed to know that.

But did they know it all? Did they also know that Lisa and Peter were really humans?

For a start it was vital for them to learn two basic things: sleeping and feeding. Lisa shuddered with fright.

They were now orcas, KILLER WHALES.

What would they feed on? Fish or mammals? Which group of orcas did their new family belong to? She was terribly afraid. Lisa did not want to mangle seals or attack other whales.

Suddenly Lanah surfaced next to her. At 22 she was fully grown and approximately 8 metres long. Compared to the other whales her dorsal fin was narrow and curved sharply backwards. It reminded one of a sickle moon.

"Lisa, are you worried about anything?" Lanah asked quietly. Lisa did not know how to phrase her question without giving away her loathing of carnivorous whales. She hesitated.

Lanah came closer. "Are you worrying about the hunt?"

Lisa was startled. How could Lanah know about this? Lisa was unable to utter a sound. "I know, at the moment there are very few fish. Until the Kas comes into the rivers we have to split up for the hunt. There are always bass. They are not as tasty as the Kas but they fill you up. You will catch some, you'll see."

Lisa was relieved. Fish eaters!

She knew bass, ugly, green-brown fish. But "Kas"? She thought very hard and finally decided to ask Peter. Slowly she swam to his side. "Have you thought about what we are going to eat?" she asked in a know-all voice. Lisa could feel Peter flinch inwardly. He hesitated with his answer. Lisa went on: "I should have known that you wouldn't think ahead! To give the all-clear: fish. They eat only fish." She could feel Peter's relief.

"You've given me a real fright, Lisa. I really hadn't thought about it. "We will hunt for bass and later for fish they call "Kas". Any idea what that means? Lanah said these fish swim into the rivers." Peter thought about this. "I think they mean salmon. They always come back to the river where they were born, swim upriver, spawn there and then they all die in the end." Lisa was satisfied with this answer. She would find out later why the orcas had a special name for salmon.

The orcas wanted to get some rest before the hunt. The children were surprised. Evening had not even come. But they felt tired themselves. To whales day and night are of no importance, as they are able to explore their surroundings with echo clicks in the dark. Therefore they had no fixed times for their dormant phases. But how does a whale sleep, who lives in the water and has to surface regularly to breathe?

"We will drown if we go to sleep!" Peter stated. "Perhaps we have to float like a *dead man*." Lisa replied. The other whales were circling them.

"It is quite easy!" Balene, the second oldest female, remarked, "We will surround you. Peter, you will swim between Manulu and Rhani, Lisa between me and Simuna. Go ahead, line up!"

Peter swam between the big Manulu and his younger brother Rhani. Lisa took her position between the two female animals. They now swam side by side, flipper to flipper. Only the two small females Jimee and Nipala huddled against their mothers' sides.

Xila, the leader, stayed in the middle, with the mighty Marete on one side and Balene on the other side forming the ends of the chain.

33

"Now you have to relax. Stay in touch with your neighbours and try to stick to our breathing rhythm. Sleep will come of its own accord." Lisa and Peter were surprised to find that the diving and breathing rhythm was totally different to playing *dead man*.

The whales inhaled five or six times and then they dived steeply. At a depth of a few metres they swam next to each other calmly. After approximately four minutes they surfaced just as steeply and inhaled another five or six times. They all kept to this rhythm accurately.

Lisa felt light and completely relaxed. The touch of her neighbours' Simuna and Balene's flippers gave her a feeling of security. She dozed off slowly without altogether losing consciousness.

Whales are able to sleep with only one half of their brain, while the other half has to control swimming and conscious breathing. Peter felt the same. For more than one hour the family stuck to this swimming formation and rested. Afterwards the children were surprised to find how refreshed they now felt.

At the same time they realized that due to the short period of rest they would need another break after a few hours.

To their surprise the catching of fish proved to be relatively easy. The whales split up into small groups and went hunting. They caught bass and trout near the mouth of the rivers. At first the other whales helped the new members of the group and caught a few fish for them. Lisa and Peter devoured this food, which they would never have touched as humans, quite naturally. They marvelled at the fact that they did not choke as soon as they opened their mouths and the seawater poured in.

But the moment they had dived a special muscle ring had closed their larynx. The entrance to the gullet, however, opened for swallowing their prey. It did not matter that they also swallowed seawater.

The whales' kidneys filter the salt and thus prevent poisoning. Whales have no need for drinking, anyway. The liquid needed by their bodies is drawn from their solid food through their digestive system with the three stomachs.

Then they started to hunt independently. It was hard to believe that they were able to hunt and kill a bass with no qualms. In this respect they were no longer human, either.

They were relieved.

Had they retained their human ideas of food they would not even have been able to take these fish into their mouths, let alone tear them to shreds and wolf them down. They would have starved.

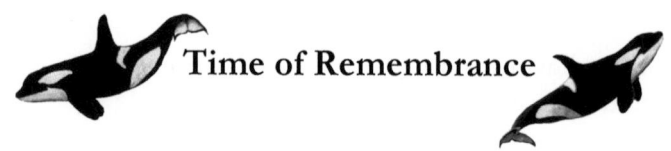# Time of Remembrance

Gradually Lisa and Peter got used to life under water. Not even the frequent rain could dampen their excellent spirits. They got to know their new and exceptional family better and better. Peter made friends with Rhani, the youngest male. Rhani and Peter were very much alike. He was a bit chaotic and rather restless. He was always up to some mischief and teased the other whales. Peter liked this. The shape of Rhani's saddle looked a bit like a jellyfish. When Rhani had teased Lisa several times she started calling him *poisonous jellyfish* or *Meduso*. Rhani took the opportunity to tease Lisa even more.

Lisa liked being near Lanah. Nipala's mother was always in a cheerful and happy mood. She always tried to ensure that everybody got on well. Lanah was one of the younger females of the group and still orientated herself quite often by her mother Balene and her aunt Simuna.

Whales take on the task of babysitters, and Simuna was the one who had often looked after Lanah when Balene was hunting.

Simuna often appeared to be sad. Lisa got the impression that she was on the lookout for somebody. In such instances she let the family move on and stayed behind. Again and again Simuna did a spy hop, raising a large part of her body out of the water. Thus she was better able to explore her surroundings above water. Simuna also seemed to be searching under water and she frequently sent out calls into the vastness of the ocean. Subsequently she listened in vain for an answer. Disappointed, she finally followed the other whales, appearing very sad and discouraged.

When Simuna once again stayed behind, Lisa approached Lanah and asked her: "Why is Simuna doing this? Is she looking for somebody?"

Lanah remained silent for a moment. Obviously it was difficult for her to answer.

"She misses her daughter Piau and her granddaughter Lesja. They both disappeared after we had lost them in a strong autumn gale. We kept looking for Piau and her little daughter for weeks, but all our calls remained unanswered. I think, Lesja must have stranded somewhere. She was still very small and inexperienced. Lesja was the same age as my little Nipala. She was exceptionally pretty and had a dark sickle in her light grey saddle, similar to my Nipala but even more distinctive. Lesja was very playful and we often had to get her out of the seaweed, as she wouldn't stop playing with the long, slippery leaves. Piau used to call Lesja with a special sound and Lesja squealed the same sound back out of the seaweed. None of us has ever used this particular sound, because it had a special meaning for Piau and her daughter, bonding mother and child. Something awful must have happened during this terrible gale. Piau would have been sure to stay with Lesja. She had already lost her first young and was very much attached to her second daughter. I am afraid they must both be dead; otherwise we would have found them. All this happened almost two years ago, but Simuna won't give up hope. She still believes in a miracle"

Lisa was deeply touched.

"This is awful! I am so sorry. Poor Simuna!"

Slowly and quietly the group continued swimming. Lisa was thinking hard. Lanah's story seemed strangely familiar. Hadn't she read something about a similar incident?

Lisa swam up to Peter and asked him, if he could remember anything. "You are right, Lisa. It all fits in with the report we read about the lost and found young whale. The dark sickle on the saddle, the distinctive call. What did they call that whale?"

"Springer", Lisa replied, "the name was Springer. Lesja could be this Springer. Oh my God, then she'd still be alive!" Peter asked Lisa to lower her voice: "Not so loud. It is possible that Lesja is indeed this whale, but we can't be sure. This would mean that we

37

are with the *Northern Resident Orcas*; between Vancouver Island and the Canadian mainland. Wow! This is cool!"

When Simuna had caught up with the family, the others surrounded her. Simuna's mother, the old matriarch Xila, did not leave Simuna's side. The other whales touched her gently with their pectoral fins to console her and show her that she was not alone. Even cheeky Rhani sought his mother's company. A great sadness had also seized him. Piau had been his big sister.

Caught up in this strange mood Xila headed towards a narrow passage, which separated the inlet, where they had stayed, from the open sea. Low tide was imminent. The mass of water, which was retreating into the sea, created a powerful undertow in the narrow passage.

"Time of remembrance", Xila said suddenly.

Lisa and Peter did not know what this meant. Xila made directly for the wildly whirling water.

"Time of remembrance!"

The current became stronger and stronger. Lisa and Peter could feel how they were pulled away by the water. But the group headed further into the current and surrendered to the power of the tides. Finally they all dived. "Time of remembrance!" The power of the water took charge. The children were full of fear as they lost control and were carried away. Wild currents enwrapped their bodies. They were no longer able to orientate themselves.

Time of remembrance.

"Seria, no!" Simuna shouted and raced towards her daughter. "No, Seria, don't eat this fish!" Simuna's voice was full of panic. Lisa and Peter did not know where they were. They found themselves in a completely different place to the one where they had been a few seconds ago. All the whales belonging to the family seemed to be younger. There was no trace of Jimee and Nipala. Strangely, the children could still feel their presence. But they were nowhere to be seen.

Simuna again shouted Seria's name loudly and raced towards the young female like a lunatic. She wanted to keep Seria from eating the dead fish. In vain. Before Simuna had reached her daughter, she had devoured the fish.

Simuna was desperate and hectically circled the young whale. Finally she butted her head gently into the young one's belly. "Spit it out, Seria! Go ahead, try! You'll get sick. The fish was rotten!" In the meantime all the whales had gathered around Seria pushing and shoving her. They all talked insistently to the young female. But it was all in vain, she did not bring up the fish.

The children did not understand the situation. Finally Peter turned to Manulu, who still gave the impression of being a teenager: "What's wrong with the fish?"

"It's dead. The fish is dead. A dead fish is not a healthy fish. We have seen flying machines going up the rivers. They were spraying something into the water. It looked like a kind of mist. Afterwards a lot of dead fish were flushed from the rivers into the sea. They're not healthy. They make you ill."

Everybody was very concerned. The family stayed close at Seria's side. After a few hours she was doubled up with pain. She was moaning and Simuna tried to console her. They were all there but unable to help.

Seria's body was convulsed with agonizing stomach cramps. Every hour she was more poorly. The whales were desperate. Finally Seria started losing consciousness for short periods of time. The other whales took turns in holding the young female above water so she would not drown. The moaning turned into a whimper.

"Don't give up!" Simuna roared. "Please don't give up!"

When night came, Seria's heart stopped beating. Her blowhole opened for the last time, but she did not inhale. Seria was dead.
*fact 1

All night long the lamentations of the family resounded in the bay. Lisa joined in the sad song. Even Peter made some sympathetic sounds. Simuna still held up her dead daughter so her lifeless body would not sink into the deep. Even though the warmth had left Seria's young body by morning, Simuna held up her daughter above the water surface all of the following day and night.

Finally Marete approached Simuna. He took the lifeless body from her and carried it piggyback to a rocky part of the bay. Peter and Lisa were surprised to see that Marete returned without Seria's body after a short while.

"This is Seria's place. Seria's place forever."

Now the children understood. The family turned round and left the bay. Simuna followed them unwillingly.

Xila increased the speed and called out:

"Seria, Seria, time of remembrance!"

There was a swooshing all around them. Lisa and Peter were pulled forward and carried along. They surrendered to the undertow and lost orientation very quickly. Eddies prickled on their skin. Tiny air bubbles whooshed past their eyes and they heard a loud swoosh.

When they regained control over their bodies they had reached the exit of the strait. The occurrences had taken place while they were carried along by the strong current. The trip into the past was over.

It was over.

Their surroundings were as before. Nothing had changed during their incredible journey. But the mood of the group had switched completely. Before there had been a depressing sadness. Now the whales were completely changed. They jumped out of the water boisterously, performed stunts and showed a happy behaviour.

Lisa and Peter were completely confused. They could still feel little Seria's presence as if she were part of the group. But Seria was dead, had died long before Lisa and Peter had turned into orcas. Old Xila approached the children.

"Be happy! You have met Seria. She is a part of us. She will always remain that. Like all the others we have lost. Nobody is forgotten. They live on through our memories of them. These times of remembrance relieve our sadness. Come on, be happy with us!"

Xila swam towards the others. Lisa and Peter followed her.

"They are completely different to us, aren't they? It makes me rather sad to think of somebody who has died. It hurts and then I miss the person even more."

Lisa startled, when Xila suddenly turned up next to her. "Lisa, things are as they are. You cannot change history, cannot bring back the dead to life. But as long as we think of them they remain a part of us, a living part even beyond death. That fills us with great joy!"

Peter agreed with her: "Xila is right. As long as memories are alive nobody is really gone, has not disappeared even if he is dead. There's something to it. I, for my part, will never forget Seria."

"Nor will I", Lisa agreed, "I am happy to have met her."

Lisa and Peter no longer felt so sad. They began to understand the whales. Together with Xila they joined the others. They let themselves be infected by the family's cheerfulness and joined them in their boisterous wild frolicking. Even Simuna had shed all sadness. They all shared a great joy, the joy of remembrance.

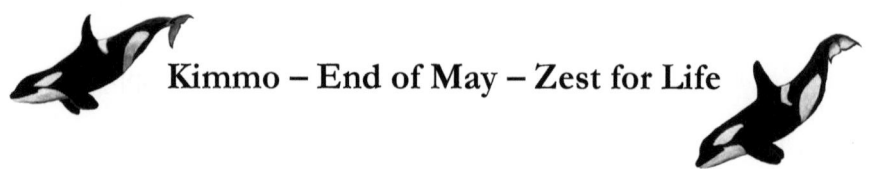

They turned up suddenly. Hundreds of them came out of nowhere. King salmon. "Kimmo! Kimmo!" the whales shouted wildly. "They are here at last," Balene remarked with relief, "now everything will become easier." Immediately the hunt for the giant fish of prey started. The family still split up into small groups. While the females Xila, Balene, Simuna and Lanah as well as the small ones Nipala and Jimee hunted near the mouth of the rivers, the males stayed in deeper waters. This made it easier for the females and the young animals to make a catch. Lisa joined Lanah while Peter tried to adopt Marete's hunting tactics.

Rhani was also still in the process of refining his hunting strategies and watched Marete and Manulu closely.

"Kimmo is the best of the kas!" Rhani rejoiced. Marete was already pursuing a giant specimen. He kept the fish, which was 1.6 metres long, in his sights constantly, either with his eyes or with his echo clicks. He did not miss a single move of the salmon.

The king salmon's skin had a light blue sheen. The back, however, showed a steel-blue colouring. The black spots on the back and the tailfin obviously had a camouflage function. Probably this camouflage enabled the giant fish of prey to pursue his prey unnoticed. The orcas, however, were not fooled by this genetic trick. Now the king salmon himself was the hunted. No fish, however well camouflaged, can escape the whales' sensory organs, which are perfectly adapted to life under water.

Marete called out loudly to the other males. Manulu, Rhani and even Peter moved forward and overtook Marete. They hurtled towards the 30 kilogram fish in a v-formation. Flight was impossible. The salmon tried an evasive manoeuvre, which brought him directly in front of Manulu's giant mouth. 48 huge teeth grabbed him. Manulu's enormous jaws clamped down and the breaking of a spine could be heard. With a few strong, jerky movements Manulu tore the fish in two. The sight reminded Peter of a crocodile. Like sharks, orcas were unable to chew their prey. Whales have conical teeth that mesh. They have only one kind of teeth. With these they can only grab, not crunch, as humans do with their molars.

Manulu left the second half of the salmon to Peter. Peter was delighted. The king salmon tasted fantastic and even half a fish was an entire meal. "Kimmo!" Peter laughed, "Kimmo!"

The seaweed was another miracle of the sea. Light green leaves with a width of up to 50 centimetres strained upwards from the bottom of the sea towards the surface. The sea had a depth of just a few metres where a forest of seaweed grew. The giant plants swayed to and fro with the current. There were many such spots. The whales loved them. Each member of the family had his or her own reason. While the elder females spent a quiet time there, swimming about leisurely, it was a challenge for Manulu and Marete, to look for especially tasty prey, which felt safe there, among the plants. The younger whales were playing hide and seek.

Rhani, Peter, Lisa and the two youngsters Nipala and Jimee, were whizzing around amongst the leaves. Visibility was sometimes down to zero, which made the game exciting for the whales. Rhani had already developed a sophisticated strategy. At first he fell back, then he weaved rapidly through the stems at the bottom of the sea and finally swam towards the other four orcas.

Lisa winced with fright, when Rhani's head suddenly appeared in front of her amongst the leaves. "Meduso!" she scolded, "you must be out of your mind! I was almost frightened to death." Nipala and Jimee giggled. This gave Rhani further encouragement and once again he disappeared behind the huge, light green curtain. Peter took up pursuit.

Lisa, Nipala and Jimee stayed together. This made them feel good. The whole thing was a bit eerie but there was no danger. This time Rhani and Peter meant to frighten the others together. Each of them approached from one side. They came closer and closer. Lisa and the two little ones swam ahead slowly. Only a few metres separated Peter from the three of them. If all went well Rhani should approach from the other side at the same time. So far the dense foliage obstructed their view.

Closer, closer. Any moment now the females would turn up behind the nearest leaf. "Now", Lisa whispered and surfaced abruptly. Jimee and Nipala did the same.

They could hear the sounds of surprise emitted by Rhani and Peter as they collided unexpectedly. Did they detect a little spark of fear in their voices? They continued playing for hours until the family moved on to hunt fish once again.

# New Moon

That night heaven seemed to open all its floodgates. It was pouring rain. Twelve hours and ten minutes had gone by since the last high tide. In a quarter of an hour the tide would once again reach its highest level.

"This time the much-water will be particularly strong", Xila warned, "We have to be careful." Peter always pricked up his ears at such remarks. He wanted to get more information. "Why will the, um", Peter was irritated, because he did not know the term *much-water*, "the much-water be stronger than usual?"

"That is due to the moon, Peter. If there is a full moon or a black moon in particular, we always get extremely high water. The difference between little-water and much-water is then particularly big. Whole parts of the coastline will then be flooded and we must be very careful where we swim. That is unknown territory. It means we could be stranded suddenly when the water goes, if we aren't careful. Stay together and keep away from the shallow water!"

Peter pondered upon Xila's words. He remembered his geography lessons. The position of the moon is the reason for low tide and high tide. When the moon is full, the earth is positioned between the moon and the sun. The moon is illuminated past the earth and is thus visible as a disc.

The exception is an eclipse of the moon, where two or three times a year the moon passes by in the shade of the earth for a maximum of 115 minutes. In case of a total eclipse the companion of the earth no longer appears white-grey but copper red to dark grey. The gravitational effect on the waters of the earth, however, remains the same. The moon is smaller but closer to the earth than the sun and therefore the gravitational force of the moon is predominant. Together with the centrifugal force, which is created by the rotation of the globe, the moon pulls the water off the earth. New moon is a different matter. In case of a new moon the moon is positioned exactly between the earth and the sun. Thus the gravitational force of the sun is increased and a maximum force is effected on the oceans. Peter was quietly happy that he was able to apply his school knowledge.

New Moon (not true to scale)

Midnight.

The water was actually there.

As predicted by Xila, the water rose a few metres higher than was usual for high tide. Tonight there was a difference of about 12 metres between low tide and high tide. The coastlines looked foreign and unfamiliar. Areas, which had been inaccessible for the whales, were now covered by the sea.

Only a few hours before this had been dry land. Where rabbits and other animals had been searching for food during the day, entire schools of fish were swimming about. Cheeky Rhani was the first to leave the family inconspicuously.

"Rhani, where are you going?" Peter asked when he noticed that the young orca wanted to steal away. "I only want to have a look. Aren't you curious?" "Well, yes. But Xila said…" "XILA. Xila is always overcautious. That's okay. It's her job. But sometimes she exaggerates. Come on!" Peter hesitated. Reluctantly he followed Rhani. At the very last moment Lisa noticed the two friends disappearing into the darkness. An uneasy feeling came over her immediately.

Rhani made for the forbidden shallow water. The water level was about two metres. It was just enough for an orca to move in. In spite of millions of twinkling stars the night was pitch-black. In places where the water surface was smooth and without waves the constellations of the stars were reflected in the water. The sea seemed to melt into the sky. The entire surroundings almost resembled the universe.

Followed closely by Peter, Rhani approached the dangerous shore area. Their bellies were tickled by grass. Carefully at first but then more and more confidently they explored their surroundings. This was indeed a different world, a world that was normally inaccessible to orcas. Peter observed familiar things but he experienced them with new senses. With the senses of a whale. Trees and shrubs were now standing in the water. He kept to himself that he had previously entered such surroundings on two legs. He could not let Rhani in on his secret. The secret that he was really a human.

Time passed quickly. Peter and Rhani were fascinated by the unusual impressions. They explored every accessible corner and ventured further and further into the flooded coastal area. They only stopped when they suddenly became aware of the other orcas' calls.

"Darn, they have noticed that we are missing!" Peter swore, "Now we are in trouble." Rhani did not seem to care. He was just crossing a particularly shallow spot and disappeared into a hollow. "Rhani, we'd better turn back. The others don't sound very pleased." The calls of Xila, Balene, Simuna and all the others did indeed have an undertone that spelt trouble.

When Rhani and Peter had not returned immediately, Lisa had alerted the other whales. The group had waited for a while to see if the two young runaways would come back of their own accord. When they did not return the others decided to search for them.

Peter was able to identify each individual call. Lisa's voice in particular was very insistent: "Peter, Rhani! Where are you?" Had he misheard? Had Lisa called out *Rhani* instead of *Meduso* as she usually called his cheeky friend? It made him think.

"Rhani, I believe they can't find us here. Let's get back to deeper waters", he begged insistently. Rhani did not answer. "Rhani, where are you?" Peter became impatient. "Damn, say something!" He approached the shallow spot but did not dare to cross it. "Rhani!"

47

Peter shouted as loudly as he was able to. Peter was torn as to what he should do.

He did not want to cross the dangerous shallow, but what about Rhani? And why did the other whales call for them so vehemently? Peter listened carefully. "Peter, Rhani! Come back! Come back immediately!" By now Peter was no longer able to distinguish individual voices. They all seemed to be calling at the same time and their words intermingled. Soon he could not understand them any more.

Xila had great difficulties in keeping Simuna from searching for her son. "You mustn't swim there, Simuna! You will only endanger yourself. The water is already retreating!" Lisa was scared. She could feel the fear within the group. "Nobody, and I mean nobody, will swim there!" Xila admonished the family. Lisa was now able to feel the low tide approaching; the water was retreating into the sea. The flooded coastline would soon turn into dry land once more. Dry land, and Peter was there. Not Peter, the human, but Peter, the whale. Lisa started to panic. So far they had received no answers to their calls. Neither Peter nor Rhani reacted. What was wrong?

Their clicks did not help in this case. The water was so shallow and the ground so hilly that the echo was literally swallowed. Lisa finally came to a decision. She could not idle away any more time, while the danger to her friends became greater and greater.
Without further hesitation she started swimming carefully into the shallow water. When Lanah saw this she shouted after her: "Lisa, Lisa! Don't!" But Lisa continued swimming: "I'll be careful, Lanah. But Peter and Rhani need somebody to warn them.

They have to get out of there." Lanah stayed behind feeling helpless. "Lisa", she whispered. But Lisa was no longer able to hear her.

Peter became nervous: "Rhani! Rhani! Cripes, where are you?" No answer. "What am I to do, what am I to do?" Peter was talking to himself. "Rhani!" By now his voice sounded desperate. Something was wrong. His body was rocked to and fro. Was he wrong in feeling that something was pulling him away from the spot where he was waiting for Rhani? He could not see anything but he had a certain feeling that things were changing.

Lisa searched for a way through the dangerous shallow water. Sometimes she had to avoid a tree that was anchored in the ground with its mighty roots. Another time she chose a way directly through some big shrubs. The branches scratched her skin but she could not afford to lose any time.

She had more and more difficulties in finding an opening where the water was still deep enough for her powerful whale's body. A depth of less than two metres was critical. She could feel the ground underneath.

Just when Peter had decided to cross the shallow spot, Lisa reached him. "There you are. Thank heavens I have found you!" she greeted him with relief.

"Lisa!"

"Where is Rhani? We must leave here immediately. The water is retreating, didn't you notice?" Only then did Peter realize what was happening. "Oh no!" he said aghast. "Rhani is behind this bump. In a minute he will no longer be able to get across. I have to go and get him." Without hesitating he propelled his black-and-white body forward with his mighty fluke and glided across the shallow spot. Lisa remained behind, shaking. "Hurry up, Peter!" she shouted after him.

Lisa waited impatiently. The minutes passed and there was no sign of the two friends. The undertow became stronger and it was very obvious that the water depth was decreasing rapidly. Where were those two? If Lisa waited very much longer she could not get back, either. Even earlier it had not been easy to find a way in from the sea. Soon it would be impossible to find water deep enough for the way back.

Suddenly she heard Peter's voice: "We're here, I've found Rhani!" "Hurry up. There's hardly enough time to get across the shallow spot!" "Don't panic", Rhani remarked placidly. He prodded Peter to make him cross the critical spot first. Peter hesitated briefly and

49

then started swimming. The ground scratched his skin. He was hardly able to move his fluke up and down. Therefore he drifted across the shallow spot very slowly. He thought he had made it but suddenly he felt a rock underneath his belly. The rock was smooth and did not hurt but lifted Peter so high that he could not move forward any more. "Help!" he shouted desperately, "I am stuck!" Lisa approached him from the front but could not help.

Peter heard a whooshing sound from behind. Then he felt a mighty push and was catapulted across the shallow spot. He carried Lisa with him. Behind him Rhani jolted across the rock and the three orcas wound up in the deeper area of the flooded coastline. While Peter and Lisa where still composing themselves, Rhani adopted his placid attitude: "I told you not to panic, didn't I?"

But the danger was not over yet. They still had to find their way back to the sea. A way, which had turned into a life-threatening labyrinth. Together they looked for a way out. They were so close to the sea, but a lot of their attempts turned out to be a dead-end. And the water continued to retreat. Out in the sea the others kept calling them and that helped with their orientation. But more than once they had to turn into the opposite direction to avoid a shallow spot or a tree.

The undertow became stronger. Rhani kept behind Lisa and Peter. He was stronger than the others but luckily not bigger. This enabled him to push the others when they were slightly grounded.

But would this always be possible?

Simuna was desperate. Was she about to lose another child? Rhani. Rhani, her second son. Lanah tried to comfort her and Rhani's older brother Manulu stayed close to the edge of the shallow water. He hoped to be able to locate the three missing orcas with his echo clicks. The two youngest orcas, Jimee and Nipala, huddled against their mothers, full of fear. But Simuna was too nervous to reassure her daughter. Jimee could feel her anxiety and sought out her grandmother Balene. At 54 she had a lot of experience and stayed calm, even though the situation was very upsetting for all of them.

They were all afraid. Afraid that the three runaways would not find their way back to the sea on time. They all knew what that would mean. They would beach. Their bodies with a weight of several tons would no longer be supported by water and their bones would break because of their own body weight. Their ribs would splinter with any sudden movement and bore into their lungs.

Should they miraculously survive until the morning, the sun would signify their certain death, because their skin would dry out. In some rare cases a beached whale managed to survive until the next high tide. But this time the water would not return in 12 hours and 25 minutes. Where Rhani, Peter and Lisa were at this moment it could take months for such another strong high tide to flood the area. There was no alternative, no plan B. They had to make it. They had to make it now … now or never!

In the meantime Marete had dared to join Manulu at the edge of the rocky coastline. They both sent their echo clicks into the flooded area continuously, while the females called the names of the missing in the background: "Rhani! Peter! Lisa!"

Low tide pulled the water, which had flooded the coast, back into the sea with all its might. In some places rivulets already trickled down the rocks. It was hardly possible to find enough water on the ground for orcas to swim in.

"Be quiet!" Manulu suddenly ordered the females. Had he heard something?

He approached the shallow water as far as possible. Manulu was 21 years old and fully grown. Like Marete at 33 he was no longer able to cross the shallow water. Their bodies were too large.

The suspense was almost unbearable. Jimee whimpered quietly and Nipala looked to her mother Lanah for consolation. Fully concentrated Marete had found a spot where the down flowing water still seemed to be deepest. The two males took their positions there. But even there the water seemed so shallow that an orca could hardly cross the spot. But in this place the three of them still had the best chance to get through.

51

It was absolutely pitch-dark. One could not see a thing. The water bubbled back to the sea through this narrow shoal. The whales remained motionless.

Out of nowhere Lisa hurtled towards Marete and Manulu. They just managed to move aside. Peter followed, but as a few minutes earlier, he got stuck. He was the same age as Lisa but his body was slightly larger and broader because he was a male. His head had already reached the sea but his belly had run aground. Again. Before Marete or Manulu were able to react Rhani sped towards Peter from behind and once again managed to move Peter forward.

But this time Rhani got stuck himself. The momentum had not been strong enough to move his body entirely across the shoal as well. Manulu approached his younger brother whose head was already suspended over deeper water. His belly, however, was stuck in the same place, which had already stopped Peter. But there was nobody to push Rhani from behind. He was the last to leave the shallow water.

Manulu swam towards Rhani's head from below and then turned towards the sea. In doing this he grazed Rhani's head and this had a pulling effect on Rhani's body. Marete imitated Manulu's actions. They now took turns in performing this tactical manoeuvre. It was extremely difficult. They must not hurt themselves on the rocks but still had to get close enough to Rhani to pull him from the shoal with their grazing movements. It seemed to work. Bit by bit Rhani slid over the smooth rock.

Eventually he managed to free himself with a strong movement of his fluke. When Rhani noticed the relieved looks of the other whales he had to laugh:

"Hey, don't you panic!"

*2

 **The Grey Whale**

The days were wonderful. Thousands of king salmon made their way into the rivers to spawn. To the orcas this meant: unlimited food. The sun shone more often than in May. The water temperature rose considerably. It was now approximately 13 degrees Celsius. Peter and Lisa were now sure. They were situated in the area between the northern part of Vancouver Island and mainland Canada. The family spent a happy time between the countless big and small islands and within the estuaries of the sea, which reached inland for miles.

Lisa and Peter soon got to know the area. Day after day they acquired new knowledge about the outline and coastal nature of the islands, about currents and water depths, about estuaries and the animals and plants under water. All the information joined together like a jigsaw puzzle. Their brain created a kind of map. However, this map contained more leads and facts than any map created by humans.

The orcas had their own names for all places. For instance the Blackney Passage with its strong current was called "Place of Remembrance". Here the water flows with a particularly strong current between Harbledown Island and Parson Island in the east and Hanson Island in the west. At high tide the Pacific Ocean pushes the water through the up to 800 metres wide passage into Johnstone Strait with all its might. When the water retreats at low tide it creates a powerful undertow out of Johnstone Strait. Here the sea has an average depth of only 30 metres. A lot of shoals render this passage extremely dangerous for larger boats. But the whales used the strong current for their own purposes: Place of Remembrance. They swam through this narrow passage regularly, but only once had they experienced a time journey.

Would it ever happen again?

Lisa and Peter thought a lot about this journey into the past. It had been a new and incredible experience. Thinking back, however, it seemed familiar and almost natural. When the others were not listening they talked about Simuna, her missing daughter Piau and her daughter Lesja, whom the humans called Springer. Piau seemed to be dead; there was hardly any doubt about it. But there was still hope for Lesja. Peter and Lisa wished fervently that the scientists could manage to return Lesja (Springer) to the *Northern Resident* whales. But they could not believe it possible. Therefore they kept their knowledge to themselves. How were they supposed to explain, anyway, HOW they came to know these things?

One sunny afternoon they met with a grey whale north of Midsummer Island. To most of the family this was not an unusual sight. Lisa and Peter, however, approached the whale up to a distance of only a few metres. Jimee and Nipala also seemed to be curious and followed them. The grey whale had a length of about 13 metres. His back was peppered with white spots. Grey whales are baleen whales. Instead of teeth they have frayed horn plates suspended from their upper jaws. Therefore they cannot bite but they filter their food from the water. Unlike toothed whales such as orcas, baleen whales have two blowholes. With a graceful movement the grey whale turned onto his right side and ploughed through the muddy ground of the ocean for prey. The water was so shallow that his left pectoral fin and half his fluke protruded from the water. It was an interesting sight. Peter, Lisa and the two young females watched with fascination.

"Can you see the baleen?" Peter asked Lisa.

"Yes, I can see them. Just watch, now he is closing his mouth and pressing out the mud. I am sure that something edible is sticking to the inside of the baleen. I wonder what he is swallowing just now." Peter laughed: "I don't think you really want to know!" Jimee and Nipala giggled. They knew what Peter meant. Grey whales feed on crabs, worms and ground-dwelling fish. Not to the taste of an orca.

54

They were swimming back south when Simuna once again fell back. The family again continued their journey slowly and silently, while Simuna sent out her heart-rending calls for her daughter and her granddaughter into the vastness of the ocean. To Peter and Lisa it seemed as if she sounded more and more hopeless each time. If only they could comfort her.

Balene joined Lisa and Peter. She sensed their restlessness but could not interpret it. "Simuna needs time. I know one tends to become impatient. We have all known for a long time now that Simuna will never receive an answer to her calls. But my little sister has not yet given up hope, and as long as this has not happened she cannot receive her daughter and her granddaughter into her memory. We can only hope that it will happen soon. She must give up searching for them. Only then we will all find peace. But we must not rush Simuna. It must be her own decision to accept Piau's and Lesja's death."

Lisa and Peter could not decide how to react to Balene's remarks. But Balene was wise enough to let her words settle. "Do you understand what I mean?" she finally asked. Peter mumbled: "Oh yes, I think I do." Lisa hesitated: "But what if Spr … Lesja is still alive after all?"

Peter shot her a warning glance. Balene did not appear to have noticed the slip of the tongue. "Lisa, Lesja would not have been able to survive without Piau. She was too young. When we lost her in the storm she was still totally dependent on Piau's milk. She was less than one year old. What gave you the idea that Lesja might have survived?"

Lisa became confused. What was she to answer?

At this moment Simuna rejoined the group. Lisa would not answer in her presence. Balene swam to the head of the group to join her mother Xila. Peter was angry: "That was a close shave! Couldn't you keep your trap shut?"

Simuna passed by and Peter fell silent. Lisa cast a sympathetic glance at the 38-year-old orca. Yes, Simuna still had three children with her: Manulu, Rhani and little Jimee. But she had already lost her daughter Seria and now she was expected to come to terms with the loss of her eldest daughter and her granddaughter. Simuna had a right to be sad. And didn't she also have a right to hope?

The Rubbing Beach

This time they did not swim through Blackney Passage on their way south. They chose the way to the west of Hanson Island. In the distance they heard the roar of ships. There is very active ferry traffic between Alert Bay on Cormorant Island, Sointula on Malcolm Island and Port McNeill on Vancouver Island. Six times a day the ferries head into Alert Bay and leave for Sointula. Twice as often the ferry commutes between Port McNeill and Sointula. The ferry routes mark a triangle.

The whales called this area "Region of Silence". The sound level of a ship's motor amounts to approximately 160 decibel. In comparison, a normal conversation between people takes place at 55 decibel. 130 decibel is the sound level of motorcar racing and jet fighters. This reaches the threshold of discomfort for humans.

For whales, who perceive the world predominantly through their hearing, this threshold is sure to be lower. Therefore they swam through the "Region of Silence" quickly and without uttering a single sound. Their heads were pounding and their bones vibrated along with the throbbing of the ships' propellers and the hammering engines. Only when they turned east below Alert Bay did the noise start to diminish. The first of the whales broke their silence.

"Shall we swim to the Rubbing Beach?" little Nipala asked her mother. Lanah whistled a "Yes". Peter and Lisa looked at each other questioningly. The whales' mood was improving by the hour. Marete and Manulu jumped out of the water exuberantly. Rhani carried out some acrobatic stunts. The females seemed to be in a good mood as well. Even Simuna turned on her side from time to time and stuck a pectoral fin out of the water. Nipala and Jimee were obviously very excited, because they breathed more often than usual.

Towards evening they reached Robson Bight. This is where the river Tsitika with its small subsidiary streams finds its way from Vancouver Island into the sea. A big river delta opened up in front of the whales, surrounded by vast areas of pebble beach.

At first Lisa and Peter did not really know what to expect. They stayed with the group of females. But when Rhani darted off, Peter was unable to resist. He propelled his body forward with mighty strokes of his fluke and followed Rhani. Lisa became uneasy: Why didn't anybody call out after those two?

As if she had read her thoughts, Lanah nudged Lisa lightly with her flipper: "Why don't you follow them? We will all join you, anyway!" Lisa did not need to be told twice. As quickly as possible she followed the two friends.

Even before Lisa had reached the two runaways she was able to hear a scrunching, clacking sound. Rhani and Peter were rubbing their bodies on the stony underground. The pebbles were clattering and rolling aside beneath their giant bodies. The two orcas were emitting sounds that were beyond doubt. This scratching action was obviously very enjoyable. Before Lisa knew what was happening she was overtaken by the other whales. Without hesitating they all joined Peter and Rhani. Lisa watched the family for a while. They appeared to be very composed and relaxed. Lisa had hardly ever seen the whales in such a good mood. Even Simuna seemed to have suppressed all her sorrows and enjoyed the pebble massage. When Lisa had watched enough of the happy orcas she joined them. When her belly touched the ground, which was covered in pebbles, she understood the others. It was lovely!

During the night other orcas turned up. They called out from afar and the family answered enthusiastically. "It's Shepee with her family", Balene explained. "We have memories in common. Listen carefully! She is with her two children and five grandchildren. What a joy!" The family awaited the arrival of the other group happily.

When they reached the Rubbing Beach there was pandemonium. They all greeted each other and grazed each other softly with their pectoral fins. When Shepee reached Xila they put their foreheads together and stayed in this position for a long time. The calm of the two leaders did not really match the wild commotion of the others' greeting ceremony.

One of Shepee's grandsons, less than one year old, was zipping between Nipala and Jimee like crazy. He pivoted and almost seemed to lose his bearings, flouncing wildly. Lisa and Peter were also warmly welcomed. No words seemed to be necessary to explain the presence of two strangers.

This was another miracle to the children. Why was their presence always so natural to the orcas? Nobody ever asked the question which they secretly dreaded: Where do you come from?

The two families spent several days together on the Rubbing Beach. Their frolicking was only interrupted by hunting and resting. Lisa heard Shepee asking old Xila: "What about Simuna? Is she still calling?"

Xila swam next to Shepee calmly. "Yes, she is still calling for Piau and Lesja. I am very worried by now. She MUST give up and allow the remembrance. Otherwise my daughter will find no peace and my granddaughter and great-granddaughter cannot be received into our memories. Their picture will fade more and more. This must not happen."

"You must talk to her soon, Xila!"

"I know. But she's not ready yet. As long as Simuna's hope is still alive we cannot take this step. I am confident that she will accept the two deaths when the kas are no longer swimming." "You may be right. The water will be colder then and it will be easier to abandon hope." "And who knows what might happen in the meantime." Xila cast a glance at Lisa and she felt caught eavesdropping.

The next morning the families separated. While Shepee guided her family to the west, Xila made for Blackney Passage. They all realized that they would go through a *Time of Remembrance*.

59

But they did not know what to expect. Lisa and Peter stayed together closely. They felt uneasy, while the others were looking forward to the event enthusiastically. "If I have understood Lanah correctly we will always be reminded of terrible things in order to come to terms with them. Why don't they ever remember nice situations? I would much prefer that."

Lisa was clueless. "I don't know, either. Perhaps it's meant to be a warning. Look, Nipala and Jimee will not eat a poisoned fish in a hurry. They know what happened to Seria. Perhaps this is their way of passing on their knowledge to their little ones."

They made for Blackney Passage. The current increased strongly. Lisa and Peter had no choice. Even though they were afraid of things to come, they had to get through them.

"Time of remembrance!" Xila's old voice resounded with unexpected force, "time of remembrance!"

Panic

They dived down to the bottom of the sea where the current was strongest. An incredibly strong undertow pulled them along, and an earsplitting swoosh clouded their senses. They lost their bearings. Inconceivable forces swept the whales along.

When Peter and Lisa managed to collect their wits, they were swimming into a lovely bay. They looked around. It was so peaceful here, downright idyllic.

How could anything terrible happen here?

Bit by bit they lost their tenseness. There were a lot of family members around them, whom they did not know, and a lot of their friends were missing: Marete, Lanah, Nipala had disappeared as well as Manulu, Rhani and Jimee. Xila was still very young, perhaps 30 years old. Her swollen belly showed that she was carrying a young. The birth was imminent. They hardly recognized Balene, she was almost an adolescent still, but she already had a young with her. But the young was not Marete.

The leap in time had to be enormous. Peter estimated it at almost 40 years. The children were watching everything closely to be able to identify the new or rather the "old" members of the family. For a start there was Lafana. She was about 11 years old and Xila's daughter. Lafana was Balene's younger sister. And there was another of Xila's children, Hou, her five-year-old son. All of a sudden Peter realized that Xila initially had had four children. Only Balene and Simuna had survived. This spelt trouble.

Balene's five-year-old son was called Zati. They also discovered Tame, Xila's sister, who was 20 years younger than Xila. At the time the family consisted of only six whales. Lisa and Peter stayed out of the way. This was not THEIR family and soon something would happen in which they did not really take part.

61

The first ship engines roared. The noise quickly came closer. The whales swam further into the bay to avoid the noise. When the boats positioned themselves behind the whales at the entrance of the bay Lisa realized suddenly: "We are trapped!"

The family swam restlessly back and forth, while the people on the boats spread a net across the entrance of the bay. Every time a whale came close they hit the water surface with some objects. The noise achieved its effect, the whale veered away every time. Xila became more and more nervous. Her youngest children, Lafana and Hou, stayed close by her side. Balene looked after her son Zati. He was a cheeky little fellow who eyed the boats curiously. The whales had no explanation. What would happen next?

Peter understood: "Oh no, they want to catch some of them." Lisa was horrified: "You mean for a marine park?"

Engines roared loudly as two smaller boats sped into the bay. They chased the whales hither and thither and finally the animals panicked. There was terrible confusion. The boats dashed around between the whales. Xila tried to shield her youngest son Hou. She pushed him under water so he would not be hurt by the approaching boat. She did not manage to reach the necessary depth herself to avoid the rotating ship's propeller.

She cried out in pain when the sharp metal edge cut off the tip of her dorsal fin. Xila's blood and her cries of pain made the orcas even more panicky.

The men on the boat shouted and Lisa registered their happy faces with dismay. What with all the confusion the orcas had not noticed a second net that had been put out. By the time they were able to assess the situation Xila's two younger children and Balene's son Zati had been separated from the others. Lafana, Hou and Zati cried for their mothers. The humans had chased them into a small corner of the bay and drawn the thin but insurmountable barrier made of net around them. Xila and Balene emitted desperate calls. Xila's fin still hurt, but her worries about the children were greater.

Suddenly there was a moment of quiet. It was only a short moment of respite, a recognition of helplessness. Then Xila, Balene and Tame swam close to the net, which separated them from their young. They were pushed away by motorboats immediately. One man hit Balene on her head with a club. But the anxious mothers did not give up. The children's cries became louder. While the three young whales huddled up to one another, smaller boats tried to manoeuvre themselves between them.

Once again the orcas panicked. Instead of the familiar body of a family member they touched the cold and shiny steel of a boat. Due to the terrible noise they lost their bearings completely and finally Hou bobbed up and down in the water motionless. Only when he felt a net tightening around his body did he strike with his fluke. Helplessly Xila and Balene had to watch as Hou was lifted from the water with a crane. Squealing with fear he thrashed around in the air and was finally lifted onto a truck. Xila and Balene did not understand what was happening.

Lisa and Peter, however, did understand. But they were only spectators of this cruel drama and not able to give an explanation, because they were so horrified.

Finally Hou's calls faded as the truck drove away from the beach. Then little Zati uttered a cry of pain. He was also caught in a net. Shortly before he was lifted from the water he thrashed around wildly and became entangled in the net.

He was now lying on his side. When his weight was no longer supported by the water his flipper bone broke. Her son's cries tugged at Balene's heartstrings. The men did not seem to care. They put Zati on another truck and drove away.

Only Lafana remained captive. At 11 years she was a bit bigger than the other two. The men had some problems with her. They tried to put the net around her body. But it wasn't as easy as it had been with Zati and Hou. After a while they became impatient. They started up the jack, even though the net did not yet supply a proper support for the whale's body. The crane wobbled when Lafana was lifted from the water. She was screaming and thrashing around. Her

63

fluke was suspended in mid-air, because the net did not support her body there. Due to her weight and Lafana's strong movements the crane teetered more and more.

It moved to the side jerkily to lift the whale ashore. Lafana was now suspended over the stony ground at a height of 6 metres. There was furious shouting amongst the men. They waved their arms about and signalled that the crane was about to topple over. Then Peter heard one of the men shouting and to his surprise he was able to understand the words: "She is too old, anyway! Cut her off!"

Before Peter could grasp the full meaning of these words one man released a fastening on the winch. Lafana plunged six metres downward, hit the stony ground hard and lay there bleeding. Her body twitched. Ignoring the badly injured orca the men dismantled the crane. They removed the nets and steered their boats from the bay. Without a thought they left Lafana behind on the beach.

It seemed like an eternity until the way towards her was free. But when the others were finally able to swim up to the badly injured whale it was too late. She was dead. Blood was spurting from her numerous wounds and tinted the water red.

Peter could not believe what had just happened. He had been aware of the fact that whales were captured for marine parks, but it was downright horrifying that the catchers acted in such an unscrupulous way. Peter hated those men and suddenly he also hated the marine parks, for whose profits the whales were captured. Lisa had followed Tame, Balene and Xila. She did not want to believe that Lafana had had to die. Her death was so pointless. Those people had just killed her, because she was useless to them.

"Too old" the man had said. And then the men no longer cared what happened to her: They had thrown Lafana away, like a useless object.

The two orphaned mothers swam around in the bay for hours without uttering a single sound. Lisa got the impression that they were waiting for Hou and Zati to return. But the children knew that they would never return.

The wound on Xila's flipper had stopped bleeding. The salt water speeded up the healing process. But Xila became more and more restless. Balene and Tame stayed close to her. Peter also noticed the change and hoped that they would soon leave this terrible place. But something else happened. First Xila was leaving a trail of blood behind her and Lisa was frightened badly. But when she discovered the small fluke underneath Xila's belly she suddenly realized what was happening. Xila was having her young: Simuna.

*3

"Lafana, Hou, Zati: time of remembrance"

It started swooshing again and their bodies were enveloped by whirls. The power of the water carried the orcas along. When they were able to perceive their surroundings consciously once again, they had reached the northern end of Blackney Passage. Peter and Lisa awoke as from a bad dream. But they were noticeably relieved when they saw all the others again.

From now on they saw Xila and Balene with different eyes. What terrible things those two had gone through! The worst that can happen to a mother is to lose a child. And Xila had lost two children in a horrible way. Hou and Zati had both been brought ashore. Even though both whales were still alive when the humans had carried them off, Xila and Balene must believe them dead. Lafana's body had been shattered on the rocks in front of their eyes. But what had happened to Tame? Why had SHE disappeared from the family?

As had happened after the last leap of time, *time of remembrance for Seria*, the family members were now completely relaxed and in a good mood. Peter and Lisa, however, were downcast. The whales had a different way of dealing with blows of fate. While humans tend to suppress appalling things, the whales refreshed their memories in a terrible way and thus found their inner peace. The children, however, felt uneasy. Not only had they witnessed this

65

awful situation, they had a bad conscience as well. They had both been to marine parks before. Never had they stopped to think where these whales could have come from. Now they saw things with different eyes: Children were separated from their mothers forever, the death of an intelligent being was approved and sometimes entire families destroyed. Sorrow and distress remained.

They were deeply distressed by the ruthlessness of humans. Did these people not know what they did to the whales? The orcas must hate humans with all their heart.

The children shuddered; they were also humans!

Balene headed for Peter and Lisa happily. "Yes, those times were terrible. They took all our young, all our loved ones, all our future. This went on for many years. As soon as we had weaned a child the humans attacked us and robbed us of our happiness. They took them away from our waters. We never saw a single one of them again. But our children were not yet independent and needed the protection and experience of the group. They are all dead! They must surely be dead!"

Lisa listened, deeply moved, while Peter carried the idea of the past further: "But you never gave up!" "No, we didn't, Peter. There came a time when they left our children alone. But we were still afraid for many years to come. Then the moment arrived when we started feeling safe again. It was all over. But an entire group of adolescents was missing. There were only old and very young animals left. Every fifth family member had been taken away or killed in the raids. With great efforts we had more young than usual. The intervals between one birth and the next became shorter and thus the families grew larger again. But the holes in our families remain until this day. We have only our memories. But is has long since been over and the sorrow belongs to the past."

The children listened to Balene's words reverently.

 The Test of Courage

They returned to their normal way of life, caught fish and still best enjoyed hunting the mighty kimmo, the king salmon, which was becoming increasingly rare.

In between they had periods of rest and enjoyed themselves on the Rubbing Beach. Finally one day the family headed north. They swam through Blackney Passage without any special occurrence. They also left Hanson Island behind them and passed numerous large and small islands. They went further and further north. They finally reached Tribune Channel and went halfway round the enormous Gilford Island.

The family dispersed a bit. Simuna and Lanah were accompanied by their small daughters. Xila and Balene ploughed through the water together, and the male animals formed the third group. Lisa was not altogether sure which group to join, when Nipala approached her and Jimee called her name. This made up Lisa's mind for her. Lisa swam off with the mother-child group. But even though the family had split up into three groups, they still stayed in touch. Several times a day they came within calling distance and made sure that everything was ok.

Peter proudly followed the two most powerful orcas of the group, Marete and Manulu. Marete was Manulu's uncle. In spite of being so closely related they did not resemble each other very much. Only the shape and colouring of their saddles showed some similarities. Their giant dorsal fins, however, were completely different. Marete's fin was very broad. It had a slight forward inclination, which was very unusual. The tip was round and sloped far backward. The fin with its height of two metres resembled a mighty sail, and with a strong wind one could see the back edge flap. On this back edge Marete had a small notch. For a long time already Peter had been asking himself where Marete might have got this wound. At some time he meant to ask. Manulu's dorsal fin was very strong and firm. It had a steep upward slope and the tip swayed backward wavelike. This fin seemed to be perfect in the eyes of the orcas. At 21 Manulu was the idol of all the young females.

While Peter was studying the two adult orcas in front of him, Rhani dashed forward. "Do you know at all where we are swimming to?" he asked playfully. Without waiting for Peter's answer he continued: "We will do a test of courage. That's cool! Manulu promised me, because Marete has finally given his consent. I am really excited." Rhani caught up with Manulu and Marete and pestered them with questions. Peter felt himself becoming more and more fidgety and brooded on this test of courage. He was looking forward to it. Finally there would be some action!

But the two male adults did not give anything away. Staunchly they maintained their course. Rhani and Peter speculated on this test of courage and kept trying to get some information from the two big ones. They were so busy trying to lift the secret that they did not notice the noise around them getting louder and louder.

Finally the noise became so earsplitting that even Rhani and Peter noticed it. When Marete and Manulu swam on, completely unimpressed, the two children became very quiet. Unbelievable that the experienced whales did not try to avoid the noise. But they did exactly the opposite; they made directly for the noise. Peter tried to get an idea of the situation. He used all his senses, jumped from the water and investigated his surroundings with his eyes and, under water, also with his echo clicks. Rhani followed his example. But Peter had an advantage: He had the knowledge of a human.

He quickly realised that lumberjacks were at work. The better part of the steep hillside was already clear-felled. In the air a gigantic helicopter was flying uphill. The rotor blades made a throbbing noise and the water seemed to vibrate. Close to the steep embankment large tree trunks were floating on the water. To prevent them from drifting away the outermost trunks were tied together. Thus the felled trees drifted back and forth within the perimeter. Suddenly the noise became louder and the helicopter came closer. Two rotors enabled the helicopter to carry enormous loads. A tree trunk, which had twice mighty Marete's length, was suspended underneath the skids with a winch. The helicopter lowered itself towards the sea. A clicking sound could be heard.

Suddenly the trunk came off its fastening as if by magic, dropped and hit the water with a deafening noise. This created a stunning shock wave. Under water the noise was almost unbearable for the whales. Still, Marete and Manulu did not budge. Peter and Rhani felt stunned and had to fight their desire to leave this terrible place in a hurry. But as long as Marete and Manulu did not leave, they had to stay as well. The spectacle was repeated every few minutes.

The helicopter came roaring down and discharged its load directly above the water surface. Each time the tree trunk dived deep into the sea, displaced the water with great force, pivoted and came back to the surface. In doing so it gained so much momentum that it once again rose from the water a bit and then slapped in again. The water around the trunk fell into chaos. First it was displaced so quickly that it carried all manner of things along. Plants were shredded, and fish lost consciousness. Finally an undertow was created each time the trunk returned to the surface as if pulled by an invisible force. Or did the sea spit out the matter, which had been forced on it? The bottom of the sea was swirled up, torn plants and disorientated fish trundled in the undertow.

It was a place of destruction.

The orcas watched the routine procedure for a while. When Marete started to move, Peter and Rhani were relieved. They expected to leave this noisy place. They were horrified when Marete did not turn off as expected but made for the perimeter. Manulu hesitated briefly: "Okay, boys … you watch first!"

With these words he followed Marete. Two completely flabbergasted adolescent orcas remained behind.

Rhani was the first to speak: "Hey, they must be crazy! What do they mean by: watch first?" Peter stared at the helicopter, which had once again started to descend. He watched Marete and Manulu diving underneath the boundary and spotted their blow within the border. Paralysed, Rhani and Peter watched what happened next. The helicopter lowered itself more and more. The rotors were already swirling up the water, where Marete and Manulu were waiting calmly. Time seemed to stop and Peter could feel the throbbing of the rotor blades like his heartbeat. Pop pop pop pop. The helicopter came even lower. Pop pop pop pop. Any time now the trunk would fall from its fastening. He saw the blow of his friends once more. Now it was Peter's own excited heartbeat, which made his body tremble. An anguished cry got stuck in his throat. Then Manulu and Marete disappeared from the surface simultaneously.

Pop pop pop. Click.

Seconds as long as an eternity went by. Had Marete and Manulu dived deep enough? Had they managed to avoid the trunk? And even if they had managed that the shock wave could have battered them against a rock or another tree trunk. Neither Peter nor Rhani were able to utter a single word. They were almost paralysed with fear.

By and by the water calmed down again. Rhani and Peter located the two other whales with their echo clicks, but could not make out their condition due to the many disturbances. Perhaps they were hurt badly?

But the two giant orcas came dashing towards them boisterously. They were in a really good mood and enjoyed the bewilderment of their two spectators. Peter and Rhani calmed down very slowly. Their heartbeat was almost back to normal when Manulu addressed them with an incredible remark: "Well, it is your turn now!"

"What do you mean?" Peter asked dumbfounded. "You're not serious, are you?" Rhani already suspected what Manulu meant by his remark. While Peter was still waiting incredulously for an answer, Rhani was already protesting: "You're crazy. I am not suicidal!" Now Peter understood as well. He considered his answer. As a rule Rhani was very courageous, even reckless. But this test of courage seemed to be too crazy even for him. Rhani turned round and swam in the other direction ostentatiously. Manulu and Marete were looking at Peter full of expectation. What should he do now? Should he dare this risky test of courage, even though Rhani did not have the guts?

There was an incredible danger of getting hurt or killed. What would Lisa advise him to do? "Well, Lisa," Peter thought. "Lisa would freak out and declare me to be completely out of my mind for even thinking about doing it." He gathered all his courage. "Okay, I'll give it a try. But you must help me!"

As soon as Peter had uttered these words he already regretted his decision. But now it was too late. Now he had to deal with it. Marete was impressed. Manulu also made an appreciative remark. Finally the three of them approached the perimeter. Some distance away Rhani had turned around, but did not come any closer. He could not believe that Peter had so much courage.

Calmly Marete, Manulu and Peter were drifting amongst the tree trunks. Marete determined the position and Manulu watched the sky attentively. Peter felt almost sick with fear. His heartbeat was so loud that he was sure he would not be able to hear the approaching helicopter. But then the helicopter was coming down from the hill. Peter was well able to hear the throbbing of the rotor blades. Pop pop pop pop. And once again a mighty tree trunk was suspended from the fastening rope. The helicopter descended. The trunk came dangerously close. Pop pop pop pop.

Peter did not hear Manulu calling and Marete's cry was also swallowed by the mind-boggling noise. Finally Peter felt the weight of two giant orcas, who were on top of him in a panic. They pushed Peter underneath the surface.

Faster, faster.

Click!

Peter was pushed to the bottom of the sea. He could feel the two friends beside, over and under himself. Everything was frantic. The giant tree trunk was much too close to him for his taste. Surrounded by air bubbles the trunk pushed aside the mass of water, forcibly burst into foreign territory, where it had no place.

"Make room!" it seemed to shout. Everything around it was pushed aside, displaced or, if it was too slow, battered. The trunk took up more space than it really needed. When it almost hit the whales its force diminished. The trunk rotated, seemed suspended in the depth for a moment and then found its way upwards, as if it had discovered its error. It did not belong here, wood floats. It seemed almost like a getaway, as the trunk rushed toward the water surface.

After just having been pushed to the ground the three whales were now being pulled upwards by an incredibly strong force. There was a spluttering and gurgling all around them and all manner of plants and animals accompanied them on their way to the top. Like a mixed group of angry pursuers everything swooshed after them. "Watch it, get out of the way!" Manulu shouted and shoved Peter for good measure. He wanted to make sure that Peter would follow his instructions. Peter reacted immediately and thrashed with his fluke as powerfully as he could.

Only with an effort was he able to free his body from the undertow. In the place where the whales would normally have surfaced with the undertow, the tree trunk hit the water surface at this very moment. Eventually Peter floated on the surface, exhausted, next to Manulu and Marete. For the two adult orcas the whole thing had been great fun. But Peter's heart was still beating wildly and the fear left him only slowly. He could still feel the panic, which had filled him when the shock wave had controlled his body and he had been unable to influence the events. Had this test of courage anything to do with skill or was it sheer luck that they had survived?

Marete was the first to start talking again. "Peter, good performance! Now let's get out of here, before the next one falls from the sky!" Peter did not need to be told twice. The three of them left the enclosed area, Peter in a conspicuous hurry. Marete and Manulu followed him. They talked quietly amongst themselves. Rhani had been waiting for them. Impatiently he had been swimming to and fro in the meantime. A number of times he had hesitated and thought about taking part in the test of courage after all, as even Peter had the guts to do it! But he had been too afraid and had stayed where he was. He had been very worried about those three. When the tree trunk had hit the water he had every reason to believe that the orcas had been hit. It had been terrible for him to be condemned to watch the happenings helplessly.

When the three whales returned from their test of courage, Rhani was still shaking. Peter joined him without a word. Peter was still scared stiff. He did not even feel very proud of having passed the test of courage; or had he only got through it?

Rhani was not sure whether to be envious of Peter or not. It was very obvious how awful the test of courage had been for Peter. "Once you've got the hang of it, it's really a lot of fun!" Manulu stated. Marete agreed: "Yes, really! A wonderful feeling to be pulled along by the water." Peter was able to guess which feeling Marete was referring to. Perhaps the panic would subside in time, once you got used to the procedure. But Peter was honest with himself. He did not want to repeat this test of courage in a hurry, fun or no fun.
*4

73

Ruthless

Marete and Manulu swam ahead. Rhani and Peter followed them at a distance. After a while Manulu pointed out an island to the two younger whales: "The humans were here and took all the trees. Now look what they left behind!"

Rhani and Peter kept lifting their heads from the water. This enabled them to have a look at the island. It was completely barren. After all the trees had been cut down the remaining vegetation was exposed to the forces of nature without any protection. Without the shade from the trees the shrubs withered within no time at all. Rain flushed the fertile soil into the sea. What remained was a wasteland. It was a bleak sight.

"Humans do such silly things. They never know when to stop. Now the island is dead. As far as we can see there are hardly any animals left," Manulu reported contemptuously. Peter kept quiet. "And now we want to show you something else", Manulu announced and increased his speed. The others followed. Finally Manulu turned into a spacious bay. Peculiar whirls pressed everything that floated on the surface into the bay almost surreptitiously. The whales were now able to distinguish strange objects with their echo clicks. They had nothing in common with the plants and animals of the sea. While Rhani approached the unfamiliar objects curiously, Peter turned away in disgust. He knew these objects only too well. Plastic bottles, containers, shopping bags, cream tins and other floating materials had accumulated in this place.

Manulu reported how the humans threw these things into the sea. They had often watched humans throw large quantities of these objects overboard. "That stuff is not like the things of the sea. It stays the way it is", Marete explained, "For many, many years. It isn't absorbed into the cycle of life like everything else here. It doesn't belong here." "Consequently it happens again and again that somebody from our world must die", Manulu added.

"A few months ago a dolphin swallowed one of these thin, larger pieces. For a moment he must have thought it could be a tasty prey. Dolphins also eat jellyfish. The strange thing must have looked very similar. When he discovered his error it was too late and nobody could help him. The thing remained inside his body and after a while he could no longer feed. His death was prolonged and agonizing." Rhani was scared by this idea. Suddenly he lost all interest in the objects. "Commit these objects to memory! They signify death!"

Slowly the orcas moved away from that filthy place. But the great amount of rubbish stayed in Peter's thoughts. Manulu had said the stuff signified death. But these were only harmless objects. Humans did not think twice about it and just threw them away. He had once left behind a plastic bottle in the forest himself, when he was out with his friends. It would have looked uncool to gather one's garbage and take it back home. But if this could signify death for the animals? He had never thought about it.

Peter decided never again to leave any garbage behind anywhere, and he would also tell his friends. It was absolutely imperative to explain to others the danger that threatened the animals through this garbage.

# The Great Gathering

After this adventure the individual small groups headed for each other and the family was together again. Lisa had spent a quiet time with Lanah, Simuna and the little ones. Excitedly she listened to Peter's stories. Inwardly she shook her head repeatedly when Peter described the test of courage in every dramatic detail. Finally he told her about the large amount of garbage and the catastrophic consequences for the animals. They both realised that the thoughtless dealings with garbage had to change immediately. Would they ever get a chance to do something about it?

It was crystal clear that they could only effect a change as humans. For the first time they wondered if they would ever change back. The thought of remaining orcas forever suddenly frightened them.

When they swam further westwards they passed several fish farms. Here the water was cloudy. Fish excrements, residual feed and fish bodies had settled metres thick. Many of the salmon within the nets looked ill.

"This is disgusting", Lisa said. "Look, some of them have escaped!" Peter was quite excited. "Unfortunately this happens again and again." Balene commented, "These creatures are awful. They carry illnesses, which they often transmit to our kas. In the year when Rhani was born there was a region where none of the big kimmos survived. The fish, which had escaped from the fish farms, had spread sea-lice. Within weeks all our kimmos died. It was awful.

Furthermore these bad fish reproduce in our rivers. They are stronger than the kas and kill their young. Thus the bad fish become more numerous and some of the kas become more and more rare. But we need the kas, because they come back to the rivers at different times to spawn and thus provide us with feed for many months. These bad fish only come for a short time and they do not taste good, anyway." Then Balene told them about a device,

which the humans had used some years ago to keep seals away from the enclosures. She told them about an ear-splitting noise, which kept all mammals at a distance and forced the animals to make long detours. "Perhaps they also wanted to chase us away. But we were never interested in these fish."
*5

When the group approached a large island, they heard the sounds of other orcas. Peter and Lisa found it hard to believe. There were about 100 orcas waiting for them. The sea was bubbling with the movements of the massive black-and-white bodies. A deluge of voices rang out from afar. It was difficult to distinguish individual voices. But after a while they recognized Shepee's calls. They sounded as happy as on the Rubbing Beach. The shape of the matriarch separated from the crowd and swam towards them. The joy of reunion was great on both sides.

Peter joined Rhani and some other adolescent whales, who were frolicking wildly in the water apart from the others. Lisa stayed in the middle of the crowd and was fascinated by the many differing bodies. The new impressions were overwhelming. Only orcas, as far as the eye could see. Lisa watched the different groups mingling. When she noticed Manulu disappearing with a splendid female she felt almost embarrassed. Lisa looked out for Marete. When she discovered him he was surrounded by females. "I'm not surprised", she thought. Then Lisa looked for Shepee's little grandson. But she could not find him anywhere.

Finally she asked Simuna. The answer was dismaying. "Many firstborn die within the first year of their life! The mother's milk for a firstborn quite often is no good. I think we pass on something sickening from our bodies to our young with the first milk. A sort of poison, which has accumulated within our bodies. With our milk we kill our own young. This is the reason why Lanah lost her son. It was so sad to see how he became weaker and weaker. Piau also lost her first young this way. My very first grandchild. This was the reason why I was so happy about Lesja's birth – Lesja."
*6

Simuna paused. Then she continued: "A long time ago things were different. But now it happens more and more often. Almost all the mothers lose their firstborn. But there is nothing we can do about it. That's the way it is. If you are really lucky your first child will survive. Piau, my first child, survived. Piau, my daughter. She survived. – Piau." With this she finally remained silent.

Lisa stayed at her side. She could feel the great sorrow, which once again filled Simuna. Should Lisa say something after all? Should she mention that there was still a small chance to see at least Lesja again?

Did it make sense to give Simuna a gleam of hope? What would happen if the humans did not manage to return Lesja, or Springer, as they called her, back here? And how could Lisa communicate her knowledge without giving away that she was human herself?

A coincidence came to her aid. In the middle of all the voices and noises she suddenly heard Lesja's name. Other whales had started talking about Lesja. Simuna joined them immediately and Lisa followed her closely. It took some time for Simuna and Lisa to understand what it was all about. There was a lot of excitement. Everybody seemed to be able to add a small piece of information, and slowly the individual parts joined together like a jigsaw puzzle. A story emerged which was virtually impossible. But several statements confirmed the incredible facts.

In the end the following seemed to be quite certain: Lesja had been spotted by several orcas, far to the south with the *Southern Resident* orcas. Initially the individual whales had not been sure. There had never been any contact between those two groups of orcas. Occasionally the *Northern Resident* and the *Southern Resident* orcas came quite close to each other further east in Johnstone Strait. But there was never any communication. The two groups had little linguistic similarities. They were strangers to each other. But still the *Northern Resident* whales had noticed this one young female orca in particular, which was swimming with a group of *Southern Residents*.

78

The little one seemed familiar. Nobody was able to explain, what was so familiar about her. When finally one of the whales, who told the story, imitated the call of the conspicuous orca it became clear that this had to be Lesja. It was the typical call, which Lesja had learned from her mother Piau.

The news spread like wildfire. While they were all talking at the same time and the fantastic news was passed on from whale to whale, Simuna became very calm and contemplative. Lisa's heart was beating with excitement and relief. Now she no longer needed to do anything and was spared the revelation that she was human.

"Lisa!" She flinched when Simuna addressed her unexpectedly.

"Lisa, you … you …", Simuna hesitated briefly, "oh, nothing. Isn't it wonderful?"

"Yes, Simuna, it is."

The meeting was now primarily used by everybody to gather all information, which the orcas had about Lesja's whereabouts. They found out about several more sightings. There was no longer any doubt, Lesja was with the *Southern Residents*, but the most important thing was: she was alive.

They talked over the various possibilities for a course of action. The longer they talked, the more questions arose. How had Lesja managed to survive without Piau? How did she get so far east? Why did the *Southern Residents* take her in?

And one question was particularly poignant: Would Lesja still recognise her family?

Lesja

It was the time of the year when the magical power of instinct drew the various types of salmon into the estuaries to their spawning grounds. Therefore feeding had first priority at the moment and took precedence over all other activities. The search for Lesja had to be postponed. Simuna could hardly wait but she had to accept that the time of abundance of fish had absolute priority. But nothing could keep her from plotting incessantly. For Lisa and Peter things were once again getting complicated.

How should they behave? The humans also had plans for returning Lesja/Springer to her family. Perhaps they would get ahead of the whales and return Lesja to her family before the whales went east.

But for the time being all whales made use of the abundance of food. Chum salmon, called keto by the whales, appeared and blueback salmon. They were called kurro. Now the children understood why salmon had the generic name *ka*. Each type of salmon started with a *k*. Kimmo, keto and kurro. Furthermore there was koho, the silversides salmon, and kasho, the humpback salmon. These types of salmon would only appear in these waters by the middle of August, when the spawning season of the king salmon was near its end. Even if the orcas preferred the kimmo there would still be enough food afterwards. At the moment there was prey in abundance. The whales ate their fill and increased their insulating layer of fat, the blubber, with these surplus calories. This thick layer of fat underneath the skin is vital. It prevents the whales from releasing too much body heat into the water and freezing to death.

The colder the water, the more insulation is necessary. With baleen whales, who are slow swimmers, the layer of fat can reach a thickness of up to half a metre. It was imperative that the orcas increase this layer of fat before the onset of winter.

But the whales thought about Lesja constantly. They all nurtured a small glimmer of hope for a reunion. And their hopes were about to be fulfilled. Rumour spread among the whales that a boat had brought an orca into the region. This whale was now said to be in a bay close to the place where the whales celebrated their *time of remembrance*. Apparently it was a young female, and some rumours nurtured the hope that she could be Lesja.

Even though this fact seemed quite unbelievable, it was established more and more through various reports by other whales. Finally Xila gave the command for departure. They had all been waiting for this and Simuna in particular was only too happy to follow the instructions of their leader.

Now there was no holding her back. Against all rules Simuna shot ahead and took her place at the head of the group formation. They were all full of understanding. Old Xila just managed to follow her with great difficulties. The rest held the usual distance quite easily. Only the two young ones, Jimee and Nipala, had to make a great effort to keep up the speed. This time the hope, which urged Simuna onward, was well founded. There was every indication that the young female orca could be Lesja. But the humans had brought her here. The humans kept the whale, who was very likely Simuna's granddaughter, prisoner in this bay.

What was the meaning of all this?

In the evening they reached Johnstone Strait once more. They quickly found the small bay, which the humans had partitioned off from the open sea with a cordon.

A lot of small boats were moving all around the bay. There were humans everywhere. Now Xila held her daughter Simuna back. "Wait, Simuna! Wait, until the humans are gone!" Simuna hesitated. But she was also intimidated by the large number of humans, and therefore the family waited at a distance of a few hundred metres for darkness to come. Even then there were still some humans in the bay. But the boats had all gone. Slowly the whales came closer to the partitioning. The net interfered with their echo clicks, and

81

they were unable to explore what was hidden in the bay. Hesitatingly they started calling out to the imprisoned whale.

At first there was no reaction. Louder and louder the family demanded an answer. Again and again the family posed the same general question.

"Who are you?" they called. They were distinctly able to discern the signs of life of the single whale in the bay. But they could not analyse them. "Who are you?" they called incessantly. Their question resounded from the bay. Xila almost lost hope that they were understood at all. Finally Rhani expressed what they all secretly feared: "What if she is not one of us at all?"

Balene snapped at him angrily for actually framing the question the answer to which they were all so terribly afraid of. For more than an hour their calls went unanswered into the bay. Then Lisa gathered all her courage and asked the family in strong terms to stop calling. Surprised by her intervention the orcas complied with Lisa's request. Lisa was quite astonished that old Xila and even the powerful males listened to her.

She swam up to Simuna and gave her a serious look: "Call her! Call her with Piau's call!" Initially Simuna was confused, but then she understood Lisa's intentions. Simuna concentrated. She had never before imitated Piau's and Lesja's call. Then she called from the bottom of her heart: "Eoe!"

Silence!

The family froze. Simuna's call resounded from the rocks and the past seemed to have returned. Xila, Balene, Lanah, every single orca sensed the presence of two members of the family, who had long since been lost. The memory was back!

Silence!

"Eoe!" it sounded very faintly from the bay. Was it a belated echo? A sound, which had possibly reverberated from a grotto with great time delay? Nobody dared to move. Their hearts seemed to stop beating. Nobody made a sound. Rhani really needed to surface for breathing. But even he delayed his actions. There was an enormous tension. Where had the call come from?

82

"Eoe!" they heard again faintly. All whales realised at this moment that this was Lesja's young voice, who answered with this very special call. Now their hearts started beating again, faster and faster until they were racing for joy. Simuna called Lesja again, first with the familiar call and then by her name: "Lesja! Lesja! Is it you? Lesja! We are here!" She added her own identifying call, which would signal to Lesja, who was talking to her: Simuna, her mother's mother!

Excitedly the orcas swam along the partition. Lesja came closer from the other side. At last it was possible to send out echo clicks. But the picture was still disturbed by the net. They were now so close to each other and still could not get together. Unceasingly they swam their laps and kept the distance as short as possible.

Lesja's answers were still full of hesitation, as if she was having difficulties in understanding the situation. Simuna also could not believe her luck. Nobody was able to ask any questions. All night long they kept exchanging calls full of joy. Finally the younger whales became tired. Lesja retired to another part of the bay and Xila and her family moved away a bit to assume their usual sleeping formation. Simuna, however, remained close to the partition.

At dawn the first boats arrived. The noise resumed in the bay. Reluctantly Simuna retired from the noise. But she stayed in close proximity. Lesja, however, approached the boats full of curiosity. Sometimes she came dangerously close. The humans opened up the partition, then moved to the side with their boats or shut off the engines.

At this moment Xila returned with her family. Simuna joined them. They all started calling for Lesja. Lesja answered and started swimming towards them. But they were not together yet. Xila did not dare to get closer to the partition in broad daylight. There were too many humans. Therefore they turned off about 100 metres before they reached the partition, hoping that Lesja would leave the bay and follow them. At first the plan seemed to be successful.

The young female left the partitioned area hesitatingly and made for the other whales. She had to cross a small stretch with seaweed. While the family kept swimming slowly, Lesja stayed within the forest of aquatic plants. She started playing with them. Simuna was the first to notice: "She's not coming! Wait!" Xila turned round and the family waited.

Boats came near. Lisa and Peter understood: The scientists wanted to see what had happened to their charge. Even though their intentions were good, their approach had a negative effect on the process. While Lesja's interest shifted from the seaweed to the boats, Xila warned her family to be careful, and thus the group removed itself to a distance of several hundred metres. In the end the humans could not prevent Lesja from accompanying the boats back into the bay.

The first attempt to reunite Lesja with her family had failed. They were all disappointed, the humans on the one side and the orcas on the other side. Only Lesja was swimming about in her voluntary prison unconcernedly and was in a good mood.

Finally darkness fell. To keep Lesja from danger and in order to be able to watch her reintroduction into the wild the humans once again closed the partition. Simuna was appalled. "Why are they shutting Lesja up once more? They already let her out."

Peter tried to explain the behaviour of the humans, choosing his words carefully. After some consideration Simuna was able to understand and accept the sense of this measure. She was facing another restless night. She would never again move away from Lesja any further than was absolutely necessary. All night long she patrolled up and down the partition, while the rest of the family was resting a bit further away, like they had done the night before. Simuna kept calling her granddaughter again and again.

Lesja answered promptly. They all hoped that the next day would bring a positive change. Lisa and Peter were able to judge both sides. The humans were hoping for success for their adventurous plans of reintroduction.

84

The whales were about to regain an important member of the family, whom they had almost given up. One could feel the tension.

The following morning the same spectacle took place as the day before. The humans opened the partition when the orca family came closer. Simuna and the others called out to Lesja and enticed her from the bay. It all looked promising. But even though they stayed closer to Lesja this time, she got caught once again in the forest of seaweed and played with the leaves. All their calling was in vain. She did not react. Simuna was close to despair, but Xila held her back once more.

Just as Lesja was swimming out of the seaweed under water, a small motorboat approached. "It doesn't work this way," Xila said. "We can't fetch her, it is too dangerous." But she had not reckoned with Lisa's determination. "Come on, Peter", she said quietly, "the scientists won't harm us. They want the same thing that we want. They are only curious. Come on!" Peter did not hesitate. When Lisa darted off he followed her with only the distance of one stroke of his fluke between them. Xila was horrified that Lisa and Peter disregarded her command. The others were almost paralysed. Only Simuna's heart skipped with exultation about the children's bold action.

Lisa and Peter, who had caught up with his friend by now, were swimming towards Lesja side by side. The engine of the small boat, which had been manoeuvred between the two and the young female, was throttled. But it kept its position. Lisa and Peter had to pass it closely to approach Lesja. The family was stunned when they watched the two orcas heading directly for the boat. The engine was cut out.

At last they reached the boat. While Lisa dived directly underneath the boat, Peter could not resist the temptation. He approached underwater and then darted from the water right next to the boat and exhaled. The humans winced and one man fell onto his backside. The boat rocked suspiciously and would have capsized, had the occupants not reacted promptly and regained their balance.

85

Peter was amused. "Let's have some fun!" he called out to Lisa. But she was preoccupied. Lesja had disappeared into the forest of seaweed and Lisa had to look for her. Lesja thought of the whole thing as a game and kept giving them the slip. It took quite some time before they managed to take Lesja between them. Apparently she still did not understand the seriousness of the situation. She kept fooling about and wanted to go on playing. But Lisa's patience was wearing thin: "Come on, Lesja! You must stay close to us! We will take you to the others!"

The children kept talking to Lesja urgently from both sides. Slowly her high spirits evaporated and the three whales left the underwater forest for the orca family. The boat was still in the same position. "I want to go there", Lesja begged. But Lisa snarled at her and Peter pushed the young female in the other direction. When they were halfway there Simuna came towards them. She uttered the characteristic call. Lesja became fidgety and finally she darted off, directly towards Simuna. At long last there was a reunion. Simuna and Lesja could not stop rubbing their bodies together. Even though their element was the water Lesja resembled a young kitten snuggling up to its mother.

Peter was happy and Lisa was deeply touched. At first the other family members held back. They waited patiently until Simuna and Lesja had finished caressing each other. It was a lovely sight, which rejoiced all their hearts. Finally Simuna and her granddaughter turned towards the others, so they could all greet Lesja.

To Lisa it felt as if Lesja was part of a jigsaw puzzle. The young female filled a painful void, a hole, which had been torn into the family by the loss of Piau and Lesja. Xila and Balene approached Simuna. They touched her flippers softly without words. Lesja was with them, but Piau was dead. But Simuna was now able to accept this and was still happy.

 # The Open Question

When the excitement of the reunion had subsided a bit, the whales swam to and fro amongst various islands, calmly and happily. The family was enjoying Lesja's presence, and Lesja herself was happy about the regained feeling of security. But more than ever before all members of the family were tormented by a question, the answer to which only Lesja could give them. What had happened back then?

None of them dared to utter this question out loud. How would the young female react when those memories, which were surely very painful, were awakened? They left the decision to Lesja, if and when she wanted to talk about it.

Just when the whales thought the day would end without the secret being revealed, Lesja started talking: "You remember that terrible storm, don't you? I stayed close to my mother as she had bidden me. She was so afraid for me. I had to make an effort to stay next to her. Even when I became more and more tired I tried my very best. But I couldn't manage any more. I fell back and my mother let you move on to stay with me.

Finally we went more and more adrift and suddenly we were in a very peculiar area. High waves were crashing against the rugged rocks and it was terribly noisy. A mighty wave grabbed me and carried me away. Mum rushed after me. In spite of the ear-splitting noise I could hear her desperate calls. I was very frightened. The rocks came nearer and nearer and I could not free myself from the power of the wave. Just when I thought I would crash against the rock and my body would be smashed, my mother flung herself between me and certain death. She screamed. The sharp stones tore her skin and ripped her right side. I don't know how she did it, but in spite of her terrible injuries she managed somehow to push me away from the rock. I reached calmer waters and miraculously survived the storm. But Mum, Mum did not make it. When it is quiet I can still hear her cries of pain and how she called with the last of her strength: "Swim, Lesja! Swim! Don't look back! Swim, Lesja!"

Simuna's heart almost broke when she heard these words. Her beloved daughter Piau's life had ended in such a terrible way. She had sacrificed herself for Lesja. All the whales were deeply touched. There could not be a more honourable way to die.

"Then I was alone. I called and called for hours. Mum would never come back. She was dead. But where were you all? I kept swimming for days and lost my way more and more. My hunger became almost unbearable. I was already very weak when another family passed by. They were like us and on the other hand they weren't. No skrutos and no tareefans. But they were none of our immediate relations, either. But I was able to understand them and they accepted me into their group. They caught some fish for me until I was able to do so myself. But I realized very quickly that I would never be one of them. One day I heard some calls and followed them. They sounded familiar. When I reached the whales I noticed that I had made a mistake. These whales were even more unfamiliar than the others and I couldn't understand them at all. It was too late to turn back. The others had already moved on. From then on I was amongst strangers, in a strange region. The only thing that still seemed familiar was the boats which were toing and froing. Their sounds were familiar and when I approached them I felt at least a bit secure. After a while I felt really awful. I was not very lucky in hunting at all. It didn't take long for me to become thin and weak."

Simuna pressed her body against Lesja to show her: You are no longer alone, you are with us!

"Then the humans came. It was strange, but I wasn't afraid of them at all. They drove me into an enclosure and made sure that the fish swam directly in front of my mouth. I recovered very quickly and felt strong again. One day something exciting happened. The humans put a harness around my body and lifted me into a small boat. I panicked at first, but the chugging of the motor calmed me down very quickly. They kept wetting my skin and caressing me. The boat kept driving around for hours. I could hear the sounds of many other boats and ships, but I could not see because my view was obstructed. When we had reached our destination the humans let me glide back into the water very carefully. Miraculously I found myself here, in another enclosure, but here. Here with you and then you found me."

Once again all the whales swam past Lesja to welcome her once more. The question had been answered. The distressing and in part amazing narrative sank deep into their memories.

*7

 **Shots**

Lesja fitted well into the group. Simuna kept her eyes glued to her. But Lisa and Peter were the ones who pushed Lesja away whenever she wanted to approach a boat. Boats seemed to have a magical pull for Lesja. She showed no reserve or fear whatsoever. The reason was probably that Lesja had had no bad experiences with ships so far, rather the opposite was true. The others knew that now.

However, there is always a risk involved for whales when they approach a boat or do not evade it. Sometimes the situation becomes downright dangerous. The ships' propellers cut through the water regardless of the consequences. The propeller blades rotate at an incredible speed. Their edges are sharp and tear up anything that gets in their way. All the whales apart from Lesja were aware of this great danger of injury. Even a boat that was steered by nature conservationists or by humans who had no evil on their minds could mean certain death for the young whale. Xila had once lost the tip of her dorsal fin this way. The sharp edge of her fin stood out as a warning to the other whales.

All members of the family were very worried: What would happen if one day they were not there in time to protect Lesja? Xila, Balene and Simuna pondered for days what to do. All arguments seemed to fall on deaf ears with Lesja. Therefore they decided to swim to Robson bight and let the "time of remembrance" work for them. Perhaps these strong impressions would cause Lesja to rethink.

Lisa and Peter were afraid of the leap in time. This time it was clear in advance that something terrible would happen. Something to shake Lesja up. It could not be anything pleasant. But the two children accepted the measure. They also wanted to prevent Lesja from approaching the boats and exposing herself to unnecessary danger.

Lesja frequently sought out Lisa and her friend. She asked a lot of questions and listened to the tales about what had happened during the past few months. But it was never mentioned who Lisa and Peter were and where they had come from. Considering all the questions this fact seemed strange to the children. But they were relieved that THIS was never a topic.

After a few hours they reached the northern entrance of the strait. But they decided to wait for the much-water, when high tide would press the salty water through the strait between the islands with an incredible force. So they remained patient for a bit longer. The excitement rose. Finally the time had come. They swam in close formation. However, only three whales could swim next to each other. Lesja wanted to join Lisa and Peter, but Simuna called her over. With Lesja on one side and her youngest daughter Jimee, who was only one year younger than Lesja, on the other side, Simuna swam towards the strong current. Peter and Lisa followed the three whales.

The swooshing started. A loud roar deafened their ears and their bodies once again lost control over their movements. They were carried along. Air bubbles interfered with their perception and violent whirls shook their bodies. Finally they lost all orientation and gave themselves over to the power of the undertow.

Time of remembrance.

Rain was pelting onto the water surface. Thick clouds were drifting across the sky. But it was neither cold nor windy. The sea was calm, with insignificant waves. The family was completely changed, as had been the case during the previous time travels. Lanah and her daughter Nipala were missing as well as Manulu, Rhani and Jimee. The children were surprised to find that Lesja was nowhere to be seen, either. Somehow they had expected to meet her. But they were able to sense the missing family members. In an inexplicable way they were also there. They took part in the events from somewhere. Why were Lisa and Peter able to see each other? They would never get an answer to this question.

The children discovered a young female next to Simuna. She was about two years old. "This must be Piau", Lisa said to Peter quietly.

They could also see an adult female with a young male next to her. He kept prodding his mother's belly with his head. The young mother was Tame. The children had already met her during their previous time travel. She was Xila's younger sister. Apparently she had still been alive during the time, which they had travelled to now.

"Pachi, leave your mother alone!" Balene scolded. "Tame, it's about time you taught him how to catch his own fish!" Tame laughed and smacked her son lightly with her fluke. Pachi started wailing exaggeratedly and kept a sulky distance to his mother. The group was amused; apparently this procedure had already turned into a ritual.

Lisa and Peter kept their distance as usual. They were fascinated by the altered family structure and by the unusual appearance of the familiar whales, who were all a lot younger.

"We must have gone back about 24 years", Peter stated. "Look, Marete is still a teenager!" The children were amazed. Balene was approximately 30 years old. Something was different about her, but the children could not guess what it was. Again and again they looked at Piau and they felt a great sorrow. Piau. She would one day become Lesja's mother. She would lose her life.

The rain subsided gradually. The whales had already heard several small ships in the area and did not appear to be bothered by them. When they got close enough to some of the boats, Lisa recognized people with cameras and binoculars. Peter read "Whale-Watch". When the tourists became too insistent, the family left the whale watchers behind and moved on. Xila was just guiding her group past a small island, when a boat approached them. At first they did not react. Their experience was that the humans would soon cut their engine or at least throttle it.

All members of the family remained calm. Even when Pachi started swimming towards the yacht curiously, the others remained relaxed. Tame, however, turned around and followed her son:

92

"Don't overdo it, Pachi. Come back!" But Pachi kept swimming defiantly. None of them recognized the danger yet.

When Lisa and Peter saw the object, which the man was holding in his hand, it was already too late. Their warning cries remained stuck in their throats and then there was a loud bang. A shot.

Pachi cried out. A second shot followed. Balene cried out.

A thundering echo reverberated from the rocky cliffs of the island towards the whales. Shrill laughter and triumphant shouting could be heard from the yacht. The children were aghast. At this moment another boat approached. The man quickly put his gun away and steered his vehicle in the other direction at top speed.

Two bleeding orcas were left behind. One of the bullets had gone through the back edge of Balene's dorsal fin. A chunk had been ripped from the fin. Pachi had been hit much worse.

The first bullet had bored into his body directly behind his small dorsal fin. It had not come out again. Tame joined him immediately and examined him with her echo clicks. The small whale was moaning with pain. The water around him turned red. Xila and the others arrived. None of them could understand what had just happened.

The other boat approached, it was full of whale watchers. Peter feared for a moment the whales might attack the small boat. He was able to see the wide-eyed humans. Horror and despair was written in their faces. But the whales were concerned with their own problems.

Balene was swimming about disconcertedly, while Tame was circling her son agitatedly. The orcas took turns in supporting Pachi from below so he could breathe at the surface. He recovered a bit and moved his fluke. The bleeding subsided gradually, but whenever he surfaced there was still blood running down his black body. Then something strange happened.

The children could not believe their eyes. Xila pushed Pachi toward the whale watch boat. Right next to it she lifted the little bleeding orca from the water. Lisa watched the humans. It was obvious that they were unable to help. At first the people in the boat were almost paralysed. None of them moved. Then one woman covered her face with her hands and started to cry. One man tore his hair and another one just sat there without moving and stared at the little bleeding whale. Finally the skipper grabbed his radio device.

After a while Xila lead the injured Pachi away. The group kept moving past the island. Pachi's gun wound seemed to settle a bit, but breathing was painful and he could not dive more than three metres deep. Balene recovered more quickly. Her injuries were only superficial. Lisa and Peter followed the family but kept their distance. Suddenly they realized what had been different about Balene before. She had not yet had the groove in her fin, which would now distinguish her for the rest of her life.

The noise of the shots and the agonized moaning of the injured whales still reverberated in the children's heads, as the family moved further and further away from them.

Then something strange happened. In an inexplicable way the sea told them, what had happened during the months after this terrible incident:

Due to his injury Pachi was unable to feed properly and acquire a good layer of fat. He became thinner and thinner. Tame befell a similar fate, because she did not leave her son for a minute. When the orcas finally started off for their winter quarters, Tame and Pachi could not accompany them. The family had to leave the weakened orca mother and her injured and emaciated son behind. They never saw them again.

The rain became stronger and soon the raindrops were pelting down on the whales so thickly that Lisa and Peter could not recognize a thing above water. They felt dizzy. There was a swooshing and they were surrounded by thousands of air bubbles. They were carried away by a mighty undertow.

"Tame, Pachi: Time of remembrance."

The Tareefans

A few days had passed since the leap in time. It was the middle of August. The whales enjoyed the warmest months of the year, particularly since it brought another bonus apart from the pleasant temperatures: an abundance of salmon. In the middle of August the spawning times of several types of salmon overlap. While the number of the popular giant king salmon, blueback salmon and chum salmon declined, more and more silver salmon swarmed towards the estuaries. The orcas called them koho.

For the orcas the table was well laid. There was an abundance of prey, and all the orcas gained a lot of weight. However, Lisa noticed that old Xila ate a lot less than the other whales. She started to worry. Was Xila ill? Her black skin appeared almost dark grey and her eyes seemed to be covered by a milky veil. More and more often she needed help to catch her prey successfully. The other whales of the family, Balene and the two adult males in particular, assisted Xila with the hunt.

In spite of this the family was in a very good mood. They had a lot of fun, enjoyed the abundance of food, frolicked about wildly in the water and carried out acrobatic jumps. Xila kept herself apart from the group more and more. Balene then took over command.

Finally Lisa gathered all her courage and asked Balene what was the matter with Xila: "Is she ill?"

"My mother ill?" Balene repeated the question. "No, why? She is only old. She has taken part in 136 migrations. That is wonderful." Lisa thought about this. Something was not quite right. Xila could never be 136 years old, no orca got that old. "136 migrations? What do you mean?"

Lisa immediately regretted her question. How could she explain why she did not know this? But Balene did not hesitate to answer: "At the beginning of the warm period we come here, and when the cold period starts we move away from here." Lisa thought about Balene's words.

Xila must be about 68 years old then. She would have liked to ask Balene where they spent their winters. But she held back. Perhaps the experienced female would become suspicious after all.

"My mother will die soon. Lisa. We all know that. She knows it herself. My mother has such great knowledge. She is a part of many precious memories. It is a great joy to see her so old. Few of us are lucky enough to go this way. Many of us leave long before their time, much younger."

Lisa was not sure whether to be happy or sad. Her feelings were all mixed up. But looking at Xila, how she turned on her back and exposed her belly to the sun with relish, Lisa's bad feeling vanished. Xila was at peace with herself. She had lived her life and was facing her end with great serenity.

All of a sudden unrest spread through the sea. Strange sounds reached Peter's ears. He heard a buzzing and whistling. It was somehow similar to their language and still completely incomprehensible. "Tareefans!" Rhani shouted. Tareefans? Peter did not know what Rhani was talking about. Lisa could not conceive what the term *tareefans* signified, either.

The noise became louder and the family swerved to the side. Whatever it was, Xila wanted to avoid direct contact. But Peter was fascinated by the situation. Manulu and Marete flanked the group and would thus swim between the approaching animals and the family. This precautionary measure made Peter even more curious. Xila would not tolerate any swerving, and the two mighty males signalled that they would enforce Xila's instructions without any doubt. Therefore Peter swam next to Manulu unobtrusively. This way he felt safe but would still see as much as possible when the action started. Lesja wanted to follow Peter, but she was held back by Simuna. She did not want to expose her granddaughter to any unnecessary danger.

The Tareefans approached with an incredible volume of noise. They made a real racket. Xila and her family were also sometimes effusively noisy, the impetuous Rhani and little cheeky Jimee in particular. But they were not used to this level of noise from creatures of the sea. Peter expected to see dolphins. But when his echo clicks reflected a picture, it showed the bodies of orcas.

"They are our kind!" he was really surprised. "No", Manulu replied, "These are tareefans!" Peter was baffled. Tareefans? Manulu realized that his answer had not been enough to satisfy Peter's curiosity. "Normally tareefans live in the deep sea without any islands. Surely they have come here for the abundance of food. So far nothing has ever happened. But we remain cautious, if only because we can't understand them. There are so many of them and you never know…" Peter stayed at Manulu's side for a little longer. *Offshores* shot through his head. The whales, who lived in the open sea in big groups, were called *Offshores*. They were hardly researched.

Like a single bulk the large group of tareefans passed the family. Their many voices created an ear-splitting noise. They seemed to ignore the family completely. Peter tried to estimate the number of orcas. He had his problems. Finally he asked Manulu. "59", was the short answer. Peter was impressed by Manulu's competence.

Peter watched the looks and behaviour of the strange whales attentively. There were great similarities to their own bodies. But the tareefans were a little bit smaller. Their fins were not as high, a fact, which was particularly noticeable with the grown males. They bent backwards a bit but on the whole had a rounded edge. Peter noticed some dolphins who seemed to accompany the group of tareefans. From this he deducted that obviously the tareefans did not hunt dolphins. They were definitely after the shoals of salmon.

Before Peter knew what was happening, the *Offshores* had already passed by. Only the pandemonium of their many voices could still be heard for some time.

Gradually things calmed down. The family regrouped. Lesja joined Peter immediately and Lisa swam close to him as well to ask a few questions. In contrast to Peter she had not been able to see much. Full of interest she listened to Peter's report about the tareefans.

 Savage Hunt

After a while something else awakened the family's attention. They noticed two whales who were looking for food in a deeper part of the sea. When Peter and Lisa swam off in the wake of the three young females Lesja, Jimee and Nipala to take a closer look at the strange whales, nobody protested. Apparently their kind did not pose any danger.

The five orcas moved away from the rest of the family. The two strange whales were about seven metres long with furrowed throats, small, sickle-shaped fins and a white stripe across their flippers. Their flukes were angular with a deep cut in the middle.

"Minke whales", Lisa stated. The smallest kind of baleen whales!" The minke whales were totally unimpressed by the five orcas. They surfaced for breathing and then continued their search for shoals of small fish. The bodily frame of the minke whales restricts their flexibility. They are less mobile, changes of direction take longer than with orcas, and in surfacing and diving their bodies are also rather stiff. This makes them radiate a sort of serenity.

The minke whales appeared almost majestic, even though they were no bigger than the orcas. Fascinated, the orcas swam their laps next to the minke whales.

However, the peaceful situation came to a sudden end. Surreptitiously another group of strange orcas had approached the group. Their scary, shrill calls made Nipala and Jimee panic, while Lesja was only slightly disconcerted. While Lisa and Peter were still wondering what these calls might signify, another ominous sound filled the water.

The children had a terrible notion: *Transients*. The kind of orcas who lived up to the name "Killer Whales". Carnivores. Not fish but other mammals are their prey. The hunt had started. There was a wild confusion straight away. Nipala and Jimee cried for their mothers. They zigzagged about aimlessly. Lesja, however, took flight amongst the two minke whales, who had recognized the danger and tried to evade the hunters.

Peter and Lisa watched six mighty carnivores approaching. They had drawn closer unnoticedly, as silent as predators. Now their bloodcurdling howls left not doubt: They were ready to attack! "Lisa, go and get Jimee and Nipala!" Peter shouted at his friend. The two little ones were completely distraught. Lisa had trouble in making herself understood. Again and again she heard the word *skruto*. Was that the term for the carnivorous orcas?

Finally she managed to make the two young females follow in her wake. The carnivores came closer and closer. In the meantime the minke whales had reached a remarkable speed.

Lesja was still between the two. She felt safe there.

But her hope turned out to be a disastrous fallacy. The supposed safety turned into a life-threatening situation. Peter followed the fugitives and had to avoid the strokes of the mighty flukes. He made for Lesja. Lisa wanted to help, but she had taken on the responsibility for Nipala and Jimee.

The attacking carnivores had almost caught up with them. They appeared aggressive and ready for anything. Their pointed dorsal fins added to this awe-inspiring impression. Innumerable scars and bitten off edges on their fins were witnesses to a hunt where the prey must have fought back desperately. The saddles behind their fins were much lighter than with *resident* whales and were sharply defined. They exchanged brief but unintelligible commands and swarmed out.

Something had to be done immediately, otherwise Lisa, Nipala and Jimee as well as Lesja and Peter together with the minke whales would be surrounded.

Lisa swung off to the left. She propelled her body with all her might and was relieved to find that Nipala and Jimee managed to follow her. They just managed to escape the encirclement. But what about Peter and Lesja?

They were surrounded. Lisa had to get help. As quickly as possible she made for the rest of the family. Lisa could have gone faster, but she had to adjust her speed to the two smaller and weaker young females. She kept urging them on: "Go! Faster! Faster!" Two of the carnivores had followed the three of them. "Skrutos! Skrutos!" Nipala shouted. Lisa felt almost giddy. She noticed that Nipala's strength was dwindling. Soon the pursuers would have caught up with them. Lisa shortly thought about falling back to protect Nipala. But then the two other females would have slowed down as well and they would not have any chance to escape at all.

Metre by metre the hunters came closer. Soon they would reach Nipala who was last. When Lisa almost expected a cry of pain from Nipala, something completely unexpected happened: The carnivores veered away.

The first reaction was relief. Then Lisa realized that they had just been chased away. They were not the targets of the attack. The carnivores, or skrutos, as Nipala had called them, wanted the minke whales, only the minke whales. But Lesja and Peter were right in the middle. Would the hunters also attack their friends?

What should she do now?

She heard a familiar voice from afar. "Lisa, Lisa! What's the matter?" Manulu was on his way to check if everything was alright. "Everything ok?" How should Lisa explain the situation to him in a hurry? She was fighting for air. Her head was pounding. Lesja and Peter were in mortal danger. The three hunted were completely breathless. Quick, quick! Lisa seemed the first who might be able to talk. She was desperate but could not manage to utter a single sound.

Her head was spinning with the various names for the hunters: orcas, carnivores.

Every second counted.

Quick! Quick!

"Skrutos!" She finally shouted as loudly as possible. Her cry filled the water and seemed to reach every corner like an ominous message. "Skrutos!"

Never before had she seen Manulu swimming so fast. He darted towards her like a torpedo. He was emitting calls incessantly to inform the rest of the family. His voice was stronger than Lisa's and the others would be able to hear him. "You stay here!" he shouted at Lisa, Nipala and Jimee when he shot past them at full tilt. Lisa hesitated. She wanted to accompany Manulu. Perhaps she could be of some help. Reluctantly she stayed with the young orcas until they had reached the rest of the family after a period of time, which seemed endless. Marete followed Manulu, while Xila, Balene, Lanah, Simuna and Rhani stayed with Nipala and Jimee. Lisa did not hesitate and joined Marete. She had great difficulties in following his strong body. The distance between them became greater, but Lisa knew that they would soon be there.

The attacking calls of the skrutos and the cries for help from Lesja and Peter, which now reached their ears, spelled something bad. Manulu's loud voice intermingled with these sounds. When Marete, followed closely by the exhausted Lisa, reached him they came across a scary scene.

The skrutos had surrounded the whales. The minke whales had surfaced to breathe. Again and again one of the carnivores tried to prevent one of the baleen whales from surfacing by pushing him down with his weight.

The mighty jaws of the carnivorous orcas were snapping from all sides. Blood was tinting the water. The whales were able to taste it. Peter had managed to reach Lesja, but they were both in the middle of chaos.

Manulu tried to approach from one side and was immediately forced back by the three hunters. There was utter confusion. Had Lesja and Peter already been injured?

The minke whales were fighting for their lives. One of them already had a gaping wound in his belly. The other one was missing part of his fluke. Wildly the skrutos kept attacking their prey. But what about the surrounded friends?

Marete joined Manulu. Lisa did the same. They only had a chance against the six greedy skrutos if they stayed together. They made for

101

Peter and Lesja. When one of the skrutos tried to push them away the three of them closed ranks and the carnivore dodged them. They managed to fight off a second attack with their strong bodies and a few powerful strokes of their flukes. Finally they broke through the ring of hunters and reached Peter and Lesja.

By some kind of miracle they had remained unhurt through all this chaos. Manulu and Marete took the three younger whales in their middle, and together they escaped. The ring of skrutos did not hold against five escapees. They burst through the wall of skrutos and were free. Lisa was surprised to find that they were not being followed.

There was no longer any doubt: The hunt was never meant for them. The skrutos were only after the minke whales, and they had been in their way.

Even so Peter and Lesja were in a state of shock. It took them a while to calm down and for a long time they kept listening to the terrible sounds that told them what was happening behind them.

The skrutos were still attacking the minke whales. Snapping sounds filled the water. The uncanny calls of the attacking carnivores mingled with the cries of pain of the minke whales. Bones splintered and tendons snapped. They were all grateful that they did not have to watch the slaughter. But the sounds were enough to make them shudder. After a while they could only hear a feeble moaning from the minke whales, until they became silent altogether.

As quickly as they could manage with their exhausted bodies, Manulu, Marete, Lisa, Peter and Lesja put a distance between themselves and the battlefield.

 **The Great Sorrow**

Utterly exhausted the five orcas reached the rest of the family. None of them had been hurt, but the shock had gripped them to the marrow. Balene, Lanah and Simuna protectively took the young whales into their midst. Little Lesja as well as Peter and Lisa needed to relax. Nipala and Jimee stayed close to their mothers. They also still showed signs of their terrible fright.

Xila took care of Manulu and Marete and listened to their precise report. Rhani stayed close to his eldest brother Manulu and listened to his words full of curiosity. At such moments he had to admit to himself that he was really still very young and inexperienced. But one day he wanted to become like his big brother. Manulu was strong and self-assured. His wide knowledge and his good looks gave him every right to be so. Manulu was Rhani's great role model.

Xila listened carefully. Occasionally she asked a question to get more precise information. Eventually she swam up to Lisa and Peter, who had calmed down a bit in the meantime and were able to answer some questions. Finally she asked Lesja why she had swum between the minke whales. "I thought they would protect me. They were so big. As big as a boat. As big as you are."

They all considered these words for a long time. Was this the reason why Lesja kept seeking the proximity of small ships? Did she feel protected by them?

Xila told the other whales a few things about skrutos: "They approach their prey quietly and unobtrusively: seals, Dall's harbour porpoises, sea birds, minke whales and even the dangerous leopard seal. There are rarely more than seven whales hunting together. They work as a team to apprehend their prey. Sometimes they are cruel and make it into a game. Their victims often die a slow and painful death. After that the skrutos shake and squeeze their prey until the poor creature has been peeled from its skin. They only eat

103

the innards. An empty animal shell remains. A shadow of its former life. Sometimes the wide open eyes still stare at you when you find such a shell."

This notion made the group shudder. Lisa was glad that she had not known this a few hours ago. She would have died of fear. Peter thought about the fact that once he would have considered this cool. In the past. When? For how long had they already been here?

Lesja snuggled up to Peter: "We mustn't forget this." Peter was confused. What did Lesja's remark refer to?

Surely she had been talking about the skrutos. He agreed with her quickly.

"The skrutos have also had terrible experiences", Xila interrupted the silence, which was full of horror. "We will remember!"

Once they had come to rest they realized how exhausted they were and how painfully empty their stomachs were. After they had satisfied their enormous hunger they rested together. Finally Xila made for the place where they were able to remember: the Blackney Passage.

"Time of remembrance!"

Once again Xila lead the family into the strong current. As soon as the enormous undertow had seized the whales, the swooshing started. Air bubbles tingled on their skins. A superior power pulled the whales along. Into another time, to another place. Soon they did not know where they were anymore. They could not control their bodies and yielded to the undertow.

First of all Lisa looked for Peter. She found him right next to her. This was as reassuring as it had been the constant during all the past time journeys. They were always together, the two friends, the humans in orcaform. Quickly they tried to recognize the present whales to establish approximately how many years they had covered in this leap of time.

Xila was much younger but already grown up. Even Balene was an adult. They were very happy to see Tame again, who was also

104

grown up at this moment of time. Simuna, however, was an adolescent. None of the young whales were there. There was only one newborn whale. It snuggled up to Balene. It took Peter and Lisa a moment to recognize this little fellow. Marete. They almost laughed. Incredible, what this half-pint would turn into.

For some reason the children knew that nothing would happen to the group this time. Not this time. But they would experience something of great importance. The taste of the water told them that they had never been in this area before. They seemed to be far to the southeast. Perhaps the habitats of the individual orca groups had changed over the years. After all, they had been taken back about 30 years.

They were passing a small bay when they heard the first cry. The sound made their blood curdle. It was the cry of pain of an orca. But it was not one of their kind, it was a carnivore, a skruto. What on earth was happening in this bay that made a skruto utter such a cry? Then there was another shrill sound. And another one. A fourth and a fifth cry took possession of air and water.

The family stayed in their position. They were about to flee. But curiosity held them back. They even thought about swimming further into the bay. Then they heard the next cry. This time it came from a different whale. There were four more blood-curdling cries. No, they would not turn into the bay. Whatever it was that was so dangerous to skrutos, what would it mean to peaceful fish eaters?

The family were almost paralysed. They must not get any closer, but they could not leave, either. Something made them stay. The hours passed incredibly slowly. They spent them as if in a fog. Their senses were dazed by the impressions of the painful cries.

Suddenly something happened in the bay. A parade of six skrutos left the *place of the cries*. Boats followed them at a short distance. The skrutos appeared completely confused. Two of them were whimpering quietly all the time.

Now Xila should have removed her group to a safe place at the latest. They had a baby with them, Marete.

A group of six skrutos could have focused on him as an easy prey. But the skrutos ignored them completely. They were filled with anguish and fear. They were cloaked in the shock of their experience. Driven by an inner force Xila examined the skrutos with her echo clicks. It seemed as if, against all reason, she had to find out what was the matter with these whales. The others followed Xila's example.

Clicks filled the water and rebounded from the six skrutos. Four of them were obviously unhurt. The other two, however, a male and a female, had strange injuries. Xila tried to explain the pictures that filled her head. She had never seen anything like this or even heard about such an injury. Peter and Lisa saw and understood, even though they did not want to believe what was revealed to them.

The dorsal fin of the approximately eleven-year-old female skruto was already fully grown, while the fin of the approximately twelve-year-old male had not yet reached its full size. Both whales had been equipped with a small box at the front edge of their fin. "Transmitters!" Peter said quietly to Lisa. "Look how they have attached them. How awful!" Lisa was unable to respond. She stared at the two injured whales and hoped that her senses deluded her. But there was no delusion, what Lisa and the others detected was a cruel fact.

Five cries from each whale.

Tack … tack … tack… tack … tack.

Five cries. Five screws.

Five thick screws had been shot through the whales' fins to mount the transmitters. Right through the middle of the thick front edge of the fin. Granted, there were no vital organs. Most likely there had hardly been any blood, either. The dorsal fin consisted of solid cartilage, similar to a human external ear, only much more solid and much thicker. Peter and Lisa shuddered. What had the humans done to these whales?

A swooshing sound started in the children's heads. Their loathing robbed them of all feeling for time and space. They were lurching around in the water, and when the skrutos passed close by them, they were carried along with the undertow. They became faster and faster. There was no stopping. Suddenly the skrutos had disappeared. They were only surrounded by bubbles and whirls.

"Skrutos: time of remembrance!"

In the present the whales were greeted by fantastic weather. The waves on the surface were sparkling and the sunbeams, which fell into the water, transformed the sea into a kind of magical world. Sharp stones reflected the light into various directions. Water plants interrupted the incidence of light and thus created wondrous patterns at the bottom of the sea.

The whales enjoyed the wonderful summer's day. Never would the water be warmer, the sun shine more powerfully. The younger whales played with their own shadows. The older ones sunbathed at the surface, always taking care not to burn their sensitive skins. Rhani, Lisa and Peter found a small forest of seaweed and played hide-and-seek. After a while little Lesja joined them. She sought out Lisa and Peter more and more often. The four of them flitted about amongst the giant green leaves. They startled and teased each other.

They all had a lot of fun this day.

In the evening the family got together again. Out of the blue Lisa asked old Xila a question: "What became of the skrutos? Did you ever see them again?"

Xila seemed to have been waiting for somebody to ask this question. "Yes, we did. We met them several times. The thing attached to their fin seemed to bother them a lot. Apparently it also caused them a lot of pain. At the end of the warm period, shortly before we went to our winter quarters, they had lost the strange objects. But with our clicks we were still able to detect hard metal parts in their dorsal fins. Each of the skrutos had five of these rods stuck in his body. The surrounding flesh was inflamed and swollen.

107

The wounds didn't heal for a long time. When we last saw them, the whales were healthy, but they had terrible scars."

"Why did the humans do this to them?" Lesja asked and turned more to Peter than to Xila. Peter felt embarrassed. He did not know how to extricate himself from this delicate situation. Why did Lesja assume that he of all whales should know the answer to her question? "Perhaps the humans wanted to check out or find out something."

*9

 Dolphins

The following days also brought wonderful summer weather. The whales frolicked in the sun-drenched, warm water. They went after salmon, which became less and less frequent. Autumn was on its way. Now and then Lesja interrogated Peter about the injured skrutos. By and by Peter gave her small, well thought out hints, which led Lesja to finding the answer to her question herself: The two boxes somehow gave the humans information about the whales' whereabouts.

Peter had acted so shrewdly that none of the others would become suspicious. Lesja informed the family about this new insight as if she had come to the conclusion herself. Peter was sure that Xila would put this knowledge down to Lesja's contact with humans.

The children still thought themselves safe from being unmasked as humans. "Just imagine", Lisa once said to Peter, when they were swimming apart from the others, "Imagine if they found out. How would they react?"

"I don't know, Lisa. Look what the humans have done to the orcas. I am sure they would despise us or possibly even hate us. They mustn't know. Never!"

Numerous whale-watch boats crossed their way. The family trusted in Xila's great experience for deciding which boats they had to avoid and which they could come close to. It was always Lesja who was particularly interested in getting close to the humans. Lisa and Peter did not let her out of their sight. And the two friends kept watching the people in the boats carefully.

"They are harmless", Lesja said occasionally. Then Peter checked the situation and mostly agreed: "Yes, they are harmless." Lisa and Peter kept looking for binoculars and cameras. They also still had the ability to read and were thus able to decide quickly when they saw a harmless whale-watch boat. But sometimes things were not quite as obvious. "They are harmless!" Lesja stated as usual, but Peter received a different impression. In most cases the ship turned out to be a private yacht. Often the boatmen headed directly for the group of whales without braking or cut them off. In such cases Peter and Lisa pushed little Lesja away from the boat.

There were days when so many whale-watch boats turned up that they disturbed the whales while they were feeding or resting. They did not do anything actively but their presence was enough to make the whales more cautious and prevented them from pursuing their usual activities. Finally Xila had had enough and they moved to a different area further north.

They were able to hear dolphins from afar. These were approaching, squeaking and squealing. They were pushing an acoustic wall in front of them like a bow wave. They became louder and louder. The twittering sounds turned into a kind of humming and hissing. The family had no reason to be afraid, they enjoyed the unusual spectacle. The sea was seething when the dolphins came within sight. Even Marete was no longer able to tell their exact number. "About 400", he guessed.

The sun was sparkling on their wet bodies. The wavy stripes on their side were an additional distraction when they shot from the water alternately. Every time one of them dived the water sprayed to all sides, and immediately another dolphin came to the surface. The water seemed to boil. Some of the dolphins executed proper stunts in the air. They pivoted or raised themselves high from the water. It was pandemonium, impossible to follow a single animal for more than a moment. If one tried, immediately five other dolphins blocked the view and – hey presto – the dolphin in question had once again disappeared amongst the mass of bodies. "I keep wondering", Balene remarked, "how they manage to find their bearings at all. Such confusion!"

They all had to laugh. There was no end to the tide of dolphins. The sea seemed to be filled with them. Body to body, each between one and three metres long. "What kind are they?" Peter asked his friend, hoping Lisa had devoted more time to this topic. But Lisa

110

was too fascinated to answer him. Or perhaps she had not heard him with all the noise going on?

She did not answer. When the last dolphins had passed by, Peter asked her once again. This time she reacted: "They were white-sided dolphins."

 **New Life**

In the meantime autumn had truly arrived. The seaweed changed its colour. Green made room for a multitude of red and yellow shades. The leaves no longer seemed like a dense forest but like an underwater sea of flames. However, for the whales the play of colours was different, as they could only distinguish shades of grey with their eyes. But even to them it was an unusual sight, as the shades of grey created by red, yellow and orange were quite different to those they normally saw.

Thus the whales enjoyed the autumnal atmosphere in their own way. Above water the same things happened as below the surface. The trees and shrubs deprived their leaves of chlorophyll and thus of the colour green.

The basic colours of the leaves remained. Yellow and red. Whole islands seemed to be aflame.

The water became noticeably colder and more and more often a sharp wind blew across the sea. Winter was almost here. The time, when the whales would leave this region, was drawing relentlessly closer. But nobody knew where they went each winter. When the others could not hear them, Lisa and Peter wondered more and more often, whether they would ever get back home.

"I am afraid, we might stay orcas forever", Lisa said to Peter one day. "Do you want to remain a whale forever?" Peter considered Lisa's question. "No, I don't want that. But what can we do to get back? We can only wait and see. I just hope they won't find out that we are humans!"

"Hush!" Lisa admonished him, because Lesja was swimming towards them. "You are so alone. So am I. Simuna doesn't understand me. She is always scolding because I go near the boats. But you understand. I know it."

Lisa nudged Lesja affectionately. "Of course we understand you. After all, the humans brought you back to us. None of the family had as much contact with humans as you." Immediately Lisa

112

regretted her choice of words. How would Lesja construe them? There was a moment of silence. "You're right, I probably know the humans better than the others." "That's true", Peter agreed. Lesja stayed with the two of them for a moment longer and then swam back to her grandmother' side.

On a particularly stormy day Shepee's group came towards them. They were all happy to meet again. "Good to meet you!" Shepee called from afar. Xila's great experience told her within seconds the reason for this remark. Her echo clicks showed her the picture of an expectant whale mother within the other group. Birth was imminent. Xila was happy. Offspring. How wonderful, how precious!

The two groups looked for a bay, which turned away from the wind. Here the water was calmer and the conditions for a birth were more favourable. Lisa could feel the great excitement amongst the female orcas. The male whales formed a protective ring around the females and the expectant mother. Rhani and Peter were allowed to join this ring, and they were proud to be allowed to take on such a responsible task. Lisa stayed in the middle with the other females, and together with Lanah and a female from the other group she was responsible for looking after the young animals. Xila, Balene, Simuna and Shepee would look after the expectant mother. It was already her third young and she was calm and composed.

The first contraction went through her body. After 14 months the little orca wanted to escape the confines of his mother's body to splash about in the vastness of the ocean.

Hours passed. Lisa looked after Nipala, Jimee, Lesja and two other young whales. It was like herding cats. While Nipala and Jimee wanted to look in on the birth again and again and got in the way of the assisting adults, Lesja made several cunning attempts at escaping. A lovely forest of seaweed was near. This still had a magical appeal for Lesja. She also wanted to get near Peter. But he was busy looking out for potential dangers.

There are some large species of sharks in this area, for whom an unprotected baby whale is an easy prey. Furthermore there were still the skrutos, the carnivorous orcas.

The birth progressed. The males widened their ring around the others to give the birthing female more room for her swimming moves. Through this she increased the pressure on the young whale inside her, relieved her belly muscles and was able to ease the pain a bit. The other females kept checking on the progress of the birth. Was everything as it should be?

Xila and Shepee communicated. Everything was ok! The other females were relieved. The good news was passed on quickly to the young animals, the "nannies" and the males in the protective ring. They were all glad that there were no complications. Each fulfilled his or her task. Their elation rose from minute to minute.

Finally a small, folded up fluke could be seen underneath the belly of the expectant mother. As soon as it had left the body it unfolded. But it was still very soft and limp. Lisa could hardly contain her curiosity. Lanah allowed her to watch the birth: "Swim over there! I can manage on my own here."

Lisa did not need to be told twice. She drew as close to the expectant mother as possible without interfering with the event. From a respectful distance she watched the little baby fluke being pushed out of the big whale body. Lisa mused why the baby whale emerged the other way round and not head first, as is the case with humans. "The tail is first to prevent the little one from breathing. As soon as the head emerges he will feel the urge to breathe. We will all have to watch out for this later on. He needs to get to the surface very quickly then."

Balene seemed to have guessed which question was flashing through Lisa's head. "Ah", she answered, slightly baffled that Balene knew her thoughts.

Contraction by contraction the small whale made his way through the narrow birth canal. The most difficult part was next, the whale middle. Even though the fin and the pectoral fins were pressed to the body it was still by far the part of the body with the

114

biggest dimensions. For a few minutes the expectant mother gathered all her strength. She knew that if she managed this effort, the rest of the baby body would emerge more or less of its own accord. By now she was much weakened by the pain. She had hardly any control over her muscles. She came to the surface to fill her lungs. She lifted and lowered her fluke rhythmically. Suddenly her movements became gentle and relaxed. Lisa felt almost frightened. For a few minutes nothing happened. The expectant mother swam her laps calmly, and without the sight of the back of a small orca peeping from her belly there would not have been any indication of this exceptional situation.

Suddenly her muscles tensed and she propelled herself forward with strong strokes of her fluke. To Lisa this came as a complete surprise. Xila, Balene, Simuna and Shepee, however, had started swimming at the same moment. While Xila and Simuna took their positions near the head of the female, Balene and Shepee stayed at an angle underneath. Now everything happened very quickly.

Suddenly the baby whale was outside. The little one reeled in his new surroundings. The cold water seemed to startle him, but instinctively he made for the water surface. Shepee assisted him by touching him lightly and stabilising his swimming direction, as his soft fins were not yet able to fulfil this function. Balene stayed directly underneath him. She thus cut him off from going downwards.

Up, up towards the vital oxygen. As soon as he had reached the line between water and air, his little blowhole opened. He took his first breath!

In the meantime Xila, Simuna and the exhausted female had turned round and swum back the short distance. Balene and Shepee immediately made room for the young mother to get to her child. In no time at all the good news spread to the outer ring of the males. Peter wanted to swim back straight away, but Marete held him back: "Not yet, Peter! In a few hours the little one will be able to swim better. Then we can welcome him." Peter was a little bit disappointed, but he followed Marete's instructions. He took the opportunity to investigate a question he had been pondering over for some time.

"Where did you get the notch in your fin?" he asked Marete bluntly.

"Well, it was really my own fault at the time", Marete explained willingly. "I used to be just as cheeky and reckless as Rhani ... and you. I used to act contrary to reason, like you, when you swam into the shallow water. In my case it was a sea lion. The others had warned me, but I thought it would be fun to tease such a creature. This wasn't a good idea at all. After all, the sea lion was half my size as an adolescent. He pounced on me with his mighty body, roaring frighteningly. I saw him tilting his strong neck backwards and snapping at me with his predatory teeth. I just managed to avoid the worst, but he caught me on my fin with one of his fangs. And gone was the corner."

In retrospect Marete seemed amused by this painful experience.

A few hours passed before Marete announced that they could all come back to the group. Joyfully they hastened to meet the newborn who was swimming next to his mother. He was less than two metres long and seemed tiny even compared to one-year-old Jimee. His fins had hardened a bit already and kept his little body stable in the proper position. His skin, however, had an unusual colouring. The black was still dark grey and the white patches were shimmering blueish-purple, which obviously looked somewhat different to the whales' eyes. Peter was surprised and feared that something might be wrong with the little one. But Marete was able to reassure him. "We all look like this at the beginning. If his mother has enough good milk, he will have doubled his weight by the time we go to our winter quarters. The blubber underneath his skin will make it less transparent and you won't see his veins shimmering through any longer. Then he will look like us. You are always worrying!"

Peter was slightly irritated by this last remark, but also relieved. Everything was ok. The little orca surfaced in short intervals to

116

breathe. His breathing rhythm was much faster than that of his older relatives because his lungs were smaller. His mother always stayed by his side but only breathed every third time. Now and again the little one swam to his mother's belly and drank the fatty mother's milk. The milk was squirted into his open mouth by conscious muscle contractions.

Balene and Xila were still flanking the mother and her newborn. They only made room for other members of the family who wanted to welcome the offspring. Every member of the two groups passed mother and child, softly touching the young whale. Thus the little one was accepted into the family. He was now a confirmed part of the family and could count on the protection and help of the others at any time.

To get rid of the tension, the younger whales jumped out of the water boisterously. The two groups were frolicking in the waves. The young mother was facing an exhausting time. Her newborn would not sleep for three months to come and nor would she. She needed the help of the entire group for her young one to survive the first crucial year. But they were all prepared to stand up for the new life in their midst and do their best.

# The Humpback Whale

During the last autumn days the water temperature once again dropped considerably. But the whales had already acquired a thick layer of fat. This had an insulating effect and the cold could not harm them. Even the little three-week-old orca did not seem to suffer from the low temperatures. He had gained a lot of weight and appeared strong. Xila was also very optimistic about the little one and decided together with Shepee that the groups would now split up again. The food supply had become increasingly poor and they needed to hunt in different areas.

There was a big farewell ceremony. The females in particular found it difficult to turn their backs on each other. But they all understood that it was necessary to hunt more successfully. They kept sending out calls to each other for a long time before the sea swallowed their strong voices.

Then they were amongst themselves once more. Jimee felt a lot older since she was no longer the youngest of the extended family. This new experience made her even more daring. But she had also just grown out of the first critical year. Jimee took on the role of the joker in the group and thus took over from Rhani, who had grown enormously during the summer. His fin had shot up and was by now very similar to the elegant dorsal fin of his big brother Manulu. Rhani felt really proud. The time had passed when he had been an impetuous, rash adolescent. HE was now grown up. HE was mature enough to go with a pretty female at the next summer meetings. HE was able to take on responsibility.

Jimee now tried to fill the gap, which Rhani had outgrown. But she was really too young for this, much too young. Her mother Simuna often had to put her in her place, when she became too cocky. Jimee was the same age at which Simuna had once lost Seria. She did not want to lose another child through its recklessness.

In the meantime Jimee's spotted back had become even more noticeable. What had shown very little at the time of her birth over a year ago was now very obvious. She did not have a saddleback at all behind her fin. In the place, where every orca has a grey or white patch, her many little light dots were just closer together. Nipala and Lesja teased her about it quite often and called: "Spotted dolphin! Spotted dolphin!" Jimee hid behind her mother each time.

Once, when she had just disappeared behind Simuna's back, sulking, a deafening call filled the sea. Immediately the curious Jimee came dashing from behind her mother's mighty body. Lisa and Peter recognized this call from various TV programmes about whales. But it was something else to hear this peculiar sound under water. They knew that this whale presented no danger at all and rushed off. They wanted to have a look.

Xila had no objections and the three young females were also allowed to leave the group and accompany Peter and Lisa. It did not take them long to reach the whale who had uttered the call. At first sight Peter's and Lisa's assumption proved to be true: a humpback whale. He was just short of 14 metres long. His pectoral fins measured almost five metres and their white front edges were shimmering under water. The mighty fluke was almost as wide as little Jimee was long, approximately four and a half metres. 28 furrows were running from his chin to his navel. Here the skin was able to extend like an accordion and allowed the humpback whale to gather an enormous amount of water in his mouth. This was necessary as the humpback whale is a baleen whale like the grey whale and the minke whale.

The orcas sent out their echo clicks to the whale to learn more about him. The whale had more than 600 baleen plates hanging from his upper jaw. At the back of his mouth the biggest plates were approximately one metre long. Peter and Lisa watched with fascination how the humpback whale caught his prey. He made a net of tiny air bubbles with air from his blowhole and thus rounded up the little fish. Then he swam towards the shoal from underneath

119

and pushed his prey to the surface with his wide open mouth. The shoal disappeared into the inflated throat pouch of the humpback whale. Subsequently the baleen whale shut his mouth and pressed the water from his mouth through the baleen plates by contracting his throat pouch and with his tongue. The fringy baleen plates acted like a sieve and held back the fish in his mouth. His prey was mainly herring, but also other smaller types of fish.

The orcas watched each of his movements attentively.

"What's this at his back?" Lisa had discovered a deep dent directly above his fluke. Peter immediately swam closer to identify the peculiar incision. "It's the remainder of a net!" he called excitedly, "The poor fellow must have got entangled in it once. He was lucky to have got clear of it. But one cord has cut deeply into his flesh."

"What's a cord?" Lesja asked promptly and Peter explained. Afterwards he wondered whether he had given away too much knowledge. But Lesja was not curious to find out. They went on watching the humpback whale.

The orcas realized that they were unable to help the big baleen whale. The artificial nylon fibre would never disintegrate. But the surrounding skin was not inflamed and had healed well. The humpback whale had probably just escaped with his life. When he surfaced to breathe a mighty fountain escaped from his two blowholes. At a height of about four metres the condensed water gathered and created a kind of cloud. After several breaths he dived again and showed his heavily humped back.

He humped his back. The children laughed: hence the name *humpback whale*. He left the "footprint" behind which was typical for humpback whales. A round glassy water surface with a diameter of five metres. Even from below the orcas were able to recognize this distinctive feature. It was formed by the steep way of diving and the undertow of the giant fluke, which had a width of more than four metres.

The orcas accompanied the humpback whale for a while. Full of curiosity they watched how he opened his mouth to gather tons of

120

water. The skin at his throat spread wide and the whale changed his looks. He seemed to be all head and mouth. It was an entertaining spectacle. The orcas were also impressed by the length of time the baleen whale was able to spend under water without breathing. 15 minutes did not seem to present any problem to him. During this time they had to surface two or three times to fill their lungs.

After some hours they left the feeding humpback whale, who obviously had not been afraid of them at any time. But how could the other whales tell which orcas were dangerous and which were not?

 **Bygone Times**

The family enjoyed the last days before the onset of winter to the fullest. They made use of the rare rays of sunshine for a warming bath at the surface and made a competition of who could still catch a salmon. There were still some fish who arrived at the estuaries hopelessly late to the delight of the orcas.

Frequently there was a thick fog above the sea, enveloping everything. Islands disappeared for days; there was no sight to speak of. The whales orientated themselves with their other senses. More and more often fierce autumn gales were blowing across the islands. Trees were uprooted and toppled into the sea. Now and again whole stretches of beach were downright ravaged. As a rule the weather did not present any problem to the whales. They swam to the lee side of an island or kept to deeper waters.

The time drew unremittingly nearer when the orcas would leave this region to go to their winter quarters.

Peter and Lisa became more and more anxious. How much longer would they be able to keep their secret? Would they find a way back into their world, the world of humans, at all once they had left this area?

They both sensed that the gate would only be open to them here. The gate, through which they would have to pass to regain their human form. But how? And if they confided in Xila, would she be able to help? Would she be willing to help at all?

They did not have much more time to think of something. "Couldn't we just ask Xila?" Lisa was getting more and more desperate. "Or we could ask somebody else, perhaps Lanah or Balene. They knew when we were coming."

"Well, yes, but they surely didn't know WHERE we came from. Or do you believe they would have accepted us? Humans?"

Lisa realized that Peter had a point. Who could know what might happen when they revealed their true identity? Lisa shuddered. Would the family turn away from them? Would they abandon Lisa and Peter or show a much worse reaction? Who could foresee this? Xila was heading for the Blackney Passage. At first the children thought she just wanted to reach the Rubbing Beach, but then Xila waited for the advancing high tide.

"Time of remembrance!"

While the other family members appeared quite relaxed, Peter and Lisa felt a rising tension.

"Nothing bad will happen", Lesja whispered in their ears, "but you still need to learn something." Lisa thought she had also heard: "before you go", but that was surely just in her imagination.

Faster than expected the current seized each one of them and carried the whales along. Air bubbles pressed against their skins. Wild eddies strained their bodies. This time the force that pulled them into the past seemed to be even stronger.

There were flickering flashes of light. Deafening noise hindered their orientation. It took forever until they were able to collect their wits.

Even the air they took in with their very first breath was different. To Peter it seemed pleasantly fresh. The children thought about this and came to the conclusion that the air contained more oxygen.

Then they began to wonder: there was no other whale in sight. This had never happened before. Where was the family? As during the previous time journeys they were somehow able to sense the presence of the others, but this time nobody was here. Had they travelled back in time so far that even Xila had not yet been born?

Confused the children looked around.

A breathtaking sight presented itself to them. There were innumerable fish all around them in the water. Most of those were unknown to them. Many of the familiar species of fish were exceptionally big. The water was clearer than in the most remote regions they had got to know so far.

And it was quiet! Wonderfully quiet. No sound of engines to be heard. Even ashore the change was very obvious. There was a rich vegetation to be found on the islands. Giant treetops stretched towards the sky. The undergrowth was also green and growing high all the way down to the beach or the rocky shore. The islands seemed to be full of life, they were teeming with animals. Yes, they had travelled far into the past this time. This was an unspoilt paradise. But where were the whales?

Lisa and Peter swam about between the islands for a while. They marvelled at the flora and fauna. It was all unspoilt by the harmful human influence. They had come to a bygone time. Long before the time of fish farms, engine-driven ships, the industrial revolution. So far they had not been able to detect a single sign of human life.

Then they heard the whales. "Eeeoooooo!" it resounded from afar. They recognized the call, they felt a familiarity, but they were listening to the calls of unknown whales. The sounds increased in intensity. Amazed the two friends listened. It was impossible to estimate the number of whales.

There had to be hundreds, if not thousands of them.

They came closer. It was an overwhelming sight. One hundred metres before they reached Lisa and Peter they scattered in all directions. They split up into groups, which consisted of many more animals than was customary nowadays. Each group comprised between 40 and 100 animals. Each group was headed by a matriarch. Apparently this had always been the case. Lisa and Peter saw animals who were obviously more than 80 years old. Nowadays it is very rare for an orca to reach such a ripe old age. Each group consisted of animals of various ages. There were many splendid males with tall fins, a great number of pregnant females, countless adolescents and a whole succession of orca babies.

The world still seemed to be in order for the orcas.

An old matriarch made directly for Lisa and Peter. She also had a large family in tow, amongst them her eldest son, whose fin overshadowed the dorsal fin of all the male orcas. It was surely more than two metres high. The matriarch greeted Lisa and Peter with a few words and asked them to follow her. Without hesitation they joined the group and accompanied them on their way.

After a while they reached a bigger island, which was obviously inhabited by humans. Peter discovered a small settlement with wooden huts. Lisa caught sight of canoes made of tree trunks on the beach. It was an Indian village. The matriarch stopped. Evening had come. The children watched the human settlement shining through the low rays of the evening sun. Soon the sun would set behind them.

Two young Indians came to the shore and navigated their dugout canoe towards the whales. They were carrying their bows and arrows. Peter felt uneasy. What did this signify? None of the whales reacted to the approaching danger. Or wasn't there any danger at all?

The orcas waited. Even when the canoe made its way through the middle of the group, they kept lying in the water quietly. Lisa meant to shout, but at this very moment an arrow swished above her head and hit the leader's son in his giant fin. The arrow had been shot off with such force that it had pierced the dorsal fin. It was now stuck, the bloody arrow tip on one side, the other half of the arrow with feathers on the other side of the fin. The whale screamed. His roar was deafening. He turned his mighty body around and made for the canoe. The other whales followed him.

The boys in their unsteady boat widened their eyes, grabbed their paddles and took flight. They propelled their canoe forward but the distance to the pursuers decreased more and more.

The strong fluke of the injured whale drove him to an incredibly high speed. With the last of their strength the hunted reached the rescuing shore. The boy who had not shot jumped from the canoe and ran straight to the village. He shouted for help. The shooter,

125

however, stumbled when he tried to jump ashore. He twisted his ankle and his Achilles' tendon snapped. The boy yelped loudly. He was now lying right on the waterline on the rocky ground, next to his canoe.

The injured whale came closer, roaring. The orca stranded, but none of the whale family seemed worried. Calmly the orca remained lying on the ground. The young Indians' eyes opened wide. In the meantime the sun was so low that the whale's fin with the embedded arrow threw a strangely shaped shadow on the beach.

The boy was filled with horror, because the shadow had the shape of a man spreading his arms. The young Indian looked up and saw a mighty figure against the glaring sunlight.

Meanwhile the entire village had rushed to the beach. Deep and powerful sounds filled the air and the water.

None of them dared to move.

The people from the village had to squint their eyes to distinguish anything, because they were also blinded by the setting sun. They saw a black outline resembling a human figure. Deeply touched the Indians listened to the eerie sounds. They sounded almost like the painful moaning of an old man. One after the other they lowered their heads, lifted their arms like the figure in front of them and started lamenting and wailing. The boy who had stumbled, stiff with fright, started to cry. Tears were pouring down his cheeks and dripped from his face. Fright made way for sheer despair. He had shot at a whale, only a whale. And now there was an injured human in front of him.

What had he done?

Suddenly the wounded orca moved and pushed himself skilfully into deeper water. The nightmare was over.

It left a people who from that day on looked upon the orcas as related to humans and worshipped them as gods.

The injured male orca passed Lisa and Peter, dashed forward and made directly for a large rock. Shortly before the collision he moved sideways, and his fin slapped against the stone at full tilt. Thus he rammed the arrow from his body. He cried out in pain and the whole group joined in the shrill sound. The noise robbed the children of their senses. Lisa and Peter felt dizzy.

Time of remembrance.

After this time journey they were in a more cheerful mood than ever. Xila lead the group to the Rubbing Beach. Shepee arrived from the west. The newborn had made good progress and appeared strong and healthy. Meanwhile his bright spots were shining in a radiant white, like Marete had predicted. It was a real pleasure to watch the little one having his first experiences with the Rubbing Beach. Lisa and Peter felt reminded of their first stay in this pleasant place.

How long ago was this?

The whales heard a ship approaching. Therefore they retreated further into the bay. Suddenly a deafening noise filled the sea. The sounds that came from the direction of the approaching ship were totally unfamiliar. There was a rumbling, metal was rubbing against metal and there was a terrible grating.

Then the whales heard some large objects hitting the water surface. Once again metal struck metal. The objects seemed to sink quickly to the ground and thundered onto the sandy bottom of the sea. The noise level and the sounds made the orcas freeze with fright.

"What was that?" they all asked nervously. None of them could explain this terrible rumbling.

"I'll have a look!" Peter called and started swimming immediately. Rhani followed him without comment. Xila and the other whales seemed too confused to hold back the two curious orcas. Even Lisa hesitated much too long with her objections about this action, and Peter and Rhani were already out of sight.

It took the orcas only a few minutes to reach the place where the terrible sound had come from. A freight ship had capsized. It was in danger of sinking. Rhani dived. "Rhani, wait! This could be dangerous!" Peter called after him. Then he followed his friend into the deep.

100 metres … 200 metres … 300 metres … the pressure on the whale bodies became almost unbearable. But Rhani and Peter wanted to solve the mystery about the strange noises. They sent their echo clicks down to the bottom of the sea.

Peter was deeply shocked, while Rhani could not make sense of the objects. But how was Peter to explain why the largest object down there was so dangerous, so terribly dangerous?

Peter studied the lost cargo as well as he could, before he had to surface. He had been able to detect eleven objects in total. The two orcas came back up from the deep totally exhausted. They exhaled with a loud noise and sucked in the fresh air greedily. They had hardly ever dived so deep before. In the region where they lived the sea was not very deep anywhere. Quite often there were only 20 to 100 metres between the surface and the bottom of the sea.

Peter had hardly recovered from the exertions of the deep dive when he made the next terrible discovery. A shimmering liquid was floating on the surface.

"Oil!" Peter shouted. Rhani did not understand this remark.

"We have to get out of here, Rhani, fast!" Peter swam back to the others, quickly but carefully. It took them a while to leave the poisonous coating on the surface behind. On the way Rhani asked some questions which Peter purposely ignored. At this very moment he did not know what to say or how to say it. Furthermore he was ruminating feverishly how he should explain things to the other whales without giving himself away.

Nobody was supposed to know who they really were, Lisa and himself.

Lisa approached the two orcas full of curiosity. "What happened?" she asked. Peter hesitated. In spite of his being very forward as a rule, Rhani seemed unwilling to give any explanations to Lisa. He wanted to be the first to pass on the news to the other whales. Lisa and Peter lagged behind. They were both relieved, as this gave them an opportunity to talk to each other freely.

"It's a catastrophe, Lisa!" Peter was very agitated.

"Tell me!" Lisa had a premonition.

"A freight ship has capsized and lost part of its cargo. Eleven large objects have slipped overboard and sunk to the bottom of the sea. The terrible thing is, apparently a tanker truck loaded with diesel is among these objects. We saw fuel on the water surface."

"Peter, wait, do you mean that the tank of the truck has broken apart?" Peter considered this. "No, down at the bottom of the sea the metal is heavily dented because the water pressure is so high, but I didn't see any holes. Perhaps the liquid on the surface did not come from the truck but from one of the large barrels. I couldn't say. At any rate, we have to get away quickly. The fumes are toxic."

There was no time to make up an explanation, because the two orca families were making directly for Lisa and Peter. The children did not know what to say. But this proved to be unnecessary. "We will remove ourselves from here!" Xila said in a serious voice and passed the two surprised orcas. Peter and Lisa joined the others without a word.

"Somehow we have to tell them that there is great danger for them", Lisa whispered to her friend. "But how?" Peter asked. Lisa had an idea. They swam up to Lesja, who, of the entire family, had the most extensive experience with humans. Lisa knew that Lesja had seen water shimmering in various colours before. She had mentioned it at some stage. With a few carefully worded sentences Lisa pointed out the danger, which sprang from the coating on the water, to Lesja.

Her trick worked. Lesja did not become suspicious but went off immediately to tell her grandmother Simuna what *she* knew about the scary liquid.

"Well done", Peter praised his friend. Lisa sighed: "If only we could do more..."
*10

The Gate

The orcas moved further north.

"We are running out of time!" Lisa implored her friend. "Something must happen soon!" Peter was still undecided whether it made sense to let Xila into their secret. This implied great danger. Finally they gathered all their courage and swam towards Xila at a quiet moment. The old matriarch saw them coming, seemed to hesitate for a moment and then joined her sister Shepee.

"Darn, now it's no longer possible!" Peter swore. "We must get her alone!" Lisa was very upset: "Perhaps there won't be another time. Peter, I'm so afraid!"

"No need to be afraid, Lisa!" Lesja had come close unnoticed. "All will be well!"

Lisa stared at little Lesja, speechlessly: "You will be moving away soon!" Peter was startled. Had Lisa just said *you?*

Tensely he waited for Lesja's reaction. "Yes, we are moving away soon. All will be well!"

With this the young orca female swam back to the other whale children, leaving two bewildered young orcas behind.

"What did she mean by this?" Lisa finally asked.

"No idea!"

The following morning they started out. It was a foggy late-autumn day, dismal and gloomy. A fine drizzle came down from the sky. It felt as if the air wanted to compete with the wetness of the sea. There was hardly any visibility above water. But this did not impair Xila's navigation. She used her echo clicks and the exact route to their winter quarters was in her head. Reluctantly Lisa and Peter joined the family. Was it too late now?

They followed the others silently at a short distance, undecided what to do. They were so lost in thought that they did not notice immediately when the family stopped.

131

Suddenly they were in the middle of the group. "We want to say good-bye!" Jimee's words sounded cheerful and completely relaxed. But this simple remark made Lisa's and Peter's blood run cold. They were unable to react in any way. They were paralysed with fear. The other whales looked at the two of them expectantly.

"Say good-bye?" Peter finally asked incredulously. Lisa was shaking. Xila came closer: "The time has come!"

"But, but…" Lisa started to stammer.

"No, Lisa, the time has come! You can't come with us. This route must remain our secret: The orcas' secret! All will be well!"

Had not Lesja used the same words? Silence fell. "All will be well!" Lanah said and swept Lisa's body with her left pectoral fin "All will be well!"

Rhani prodded Peter with the tip of his snout. "All will be well!" All the others caressed Lisa and Peter. From all sides these words reached their ears, and tender touches took away their fear. "All will be well!"

Then the family broke away from Lisa and Peter and followed Xila, who had started on their way to the unknown winter quarters. Lesja paused once more, turned around towards the children: "All will be well! Believe me!"

Without a word the children followed the whales, who were moving away, with their eyes. They were their friends, who were departing, even more, they were their family. The rain was pattering onto the water and the familiar outlines became more and more blurred, until even Lesja's little whale body was swallowed up by the murky sea.

"We have to tell you something!" Peter shouted suddenly. His call resounded from the rocky shore and the echoes seemed to fill the entire sea.

"We have to tell you something!"
"We have to tell you something!"
"have to tell you something!"
"to tell you something!"

"tell you something!"
   "something!"

"Eeeoooooo"
A familiar call reached their ears.

"Eeeoooooo"
The echo distorted the sounds.

"Weeeooooo!"
   "Weeee eeeoooo!"
   "We neooo!"
   "We knew!"

"We knew!"

The words befogged their senses. The family knew! They knew! They had known all the time, known, that Lisa and Peter were humans and had still accepted them. They had known and still let them into deep secrets of the whales. They had known and allowed Lisa and Peter, humans, to become part of their family.

They had known and therefore had to keep their last secret: Where the orcas go for the winter. But they had shown them so many things. They had wanted the humans to learn so much.

They knew!

This insight enwrapped the children like a bright veil. It befogged their senses. They felt light and beyond time and space. Were they still in the water? They could not feel a thing. They could not see a thing. They were floating. Somewhere! Nowhere?

No, they were halfway through the gate already.

A light flashed. A loud noise wrenched them from the no-man's-space, which was filled with wafts of mist and literally catapulted them through the last part of the gate.

133

They knew!
All will be well!

It was dark. Pitch-dark. A swooshing filled the room. The room? Lightning flashed and almost at the same time thunder rolled and passed through the children's bodies. The room. They were back in Lisa's room. When the next lightning flashed they looked at their bodies. Arms, legs. They had turned back into humans. They could hardly believe it. Then the light started flickering and finally the current entry was constant enough for the light to stay on. Lisa and Peter hugged each other. They were cheering. A moment later they realised the embarrassing situation and let go of each other. After all, they were now human again.

Epilogue

The following day Lisa and Peter gave their talk about the topic: *killer whales.*

They did not need any notes, no poster, not even the CD with the calls of the whales.

The memories of their incredible experiences were the only thing that was necessary. Their descriptions filled the classroom, they stimulated the imagination of their classmates, they overruled the reason of all their listeners, they made time and space lose their importance. Their explanations were so precise, their descriptions so impressive and spellbinding that the whole audience came to know the world of the orcas from a different perspective, saw it through different eyes:

Through the eyes of the orcas!

When the bell rang and announced the end of the school day, the teacher and the pupils hesitated to leave the classroom. None of them spoke a single word. But they all felt the power of the forces of nature in an inexplicable way, felt the water on their skins, sensed an enormous familiarity with the orcas, and long after the presentation they still heard the call which explained everything:

"Eeeeoooooooooooooo!"

Facts:

*1

1998 herbicides (weed killers) are sprayed over some rivers by plane: Afterwards the rivers Keogh, Nimpkish, Suquash, Nahwitti and Stranby are without salmon.

*2

1980 some whales swim into a flooded meadow.

*3

1962-1977 in British Columbia and Washington between 275 and 307 orcas are caught altogether. Weaned young animals are the target (easier to train). 11 die, 56 are kept for dolphinariums, the rest is set free. In general 75% of the dolphins caught for dolphinariums die either during transport or shortly afterwards.

1971 a census is finally initiated. Michael Bigg and Graeme M. Ellis estimate the population in this area between 200 and 250 orcas. Approximately 1/5 of the entire population was captured or killed. All whales, which had been born between 1960 and 1970, were captured.

*4

In her book "Listening to Whales" Alexandra Morton describes the following observation:

"Orcas swim into the roped-off area where tree trunks are dropped by helicopters. They re-surface with a fish in their mouth."

*5

Aquacultures/fish farms:

The number of fish farms along the coastline of B.C. in 2007 amounts to 134 net pens. Their size is approximately 30 m in diameter. Their depth varies between six and 20 metres. Each pen comprises between 35,000 and 50,000 fish. More than half of these fish farms breed the

Atlantic salmon, which is not at home in the waters of the Pacific. This type of salmon was chosen for the following reasons:
1. It grows faster and has a higher survival rate than the Pacific salmon.
2. There is a bigger market for the Atlantic salmon.
3. It produces more meat, less waste is left over from the fish.
In 2005 these farms produced 98.441 tons of fish. The value of these salmon amounts to $543,634,000. Canada thus holds a share of 6% of the worldwide salmon production. 95 % of the fish bred in Canadian salmon farms are exported to the USA. Since 1991 around 452,049 Atlantic salmon have escaped from the farms according to official statements (up to 2002). (Footnote: The dark figure amounts to a number many times over.) According to the Canadian Ministry of Fisheries and Oceans the escaped Atlantic salmon do not pose any threat to the native salmon population.
(Source: Canada - Minister of Fisheries and Oceans, www.dfo-mpo.ca)
Counter statement by the following source: KNU (Koordinationszentrum Natur und Umwelt e.V.) www.naturschatz.org with quotes by Martin Krkosek, Mark A. Lewis, John P.l Volpe, Unversitiy of Alberta Edmonton "Proceedings of the Royal Society of London B"
"...Young fish were hardly afflicted with sea lice before they came into the vicinity of the fish farm. This changed rapidly in the waters around the salmon farm. The concentration of parasites was a 30,000-fold higher around the fish farm than in other waters..."
"...Adult salmon normally survive the infestation with sea lice. But fish, which are only a few days old, cannot tolerate the parasites. The sea lice eat more than their hosts, which are thus consumed alive."
" ... Due to the high stocking rate in the freely floating pens illnesses can spread rapidly. Therefore the following chemical cocktail is added to the water:
- Antibiotics against bacteria and viruses
- Fungicides ... against mycoses
- Pesticides against fish parasites such as sea lice

- Dyes … to ensure that the salmon meat gets its characteristic colour
- Furthermore young salmon are automatically injected with growth hormones…"

Current state of affairs:

May 2007 a government committee advises abolition of open net pens and cessation of permits for aquacultures – fish farms along the migratory routes of spawning salmon should disappear and be permanently prohibited north of Cape Caution – the implementation of this recommendation is doubtful.

Quoting Alexandra Morton www.raincoastresearch.org:

"Wherever there are salmon farms, there have been epidemic outbreaks of the salmon-specific salmon louse *Lepeophtheirus salmonis*.... Wild Pacific salmon become infected with sea lice in the open ocean."

Webpage www.orcalab.org by A. Spong

"The young salmon are at their most vulnerable stage (author's note: when passing the salmon farms), and the lice challenge them at levels they are not able to survive. As a result, the salmon runs of the Broughton are crashing."

1993 Eastern part of the Fife Sound. The so-called "pinger" is used. This "acoustic broom" has a sound level of 194 decibel (140 decibel is the absolute threshold of pain for humans).

*6

Quoting the WWF-expert Karoline Schacht about the high concentration of pollutants found in Norwegian orcas (Dec. 2005):

"The alarming results show, how poorly the habitat sea is doing. The orcas are at the end of the food chain. They reflect the alarming spreading of industrial chemicals."

Quoting WDCS (Whale and Dolphin Conservation Society) from Associated Press (Oct. 2002):

"A toxic chemical, which may devastate the development of young whale calves has been found in high concentrations in the blubber of a Monterey Bay killer whale."

138

Quoting WDCS from L.A. Times dated 2001/02/16:
"According to scientific studies some of the orcas living in the coastal waters off Washington State, British Columbia, Canada and South-central Alaska have accumulated dangerously high concentrations of industrial chemicals (PCB and DDT). ... The passing on of PCB's through the mothers' milk is particularly alarming. Since PCB's block the production of vitamin A, an important hormone they are very likely to have a negative effect on the development and the survival rate of the calves. Furthermore it has been known for quite some time that high concentrations of PCB can weaken the immune system of animals."

Quote from the webpage ,Meeresakrobaten' (acrobats of the sea):
"The mortality rate is relatively high. Only about 60 percent of the calves become older than one year."

*7

Springer

(Scientific name A73) - female

She is born in July 2000 as the second young of Sutlej (A45). Sutlej's first calf died in its first year. In autumn 2000 Springer is seen together with her mother for the last time. In summer 2001 Springer is swimming without her mother. She is accompanying orcas from the G-pod, which is very unusual. In January 2002 Springer turns up in Puget Sound, which counts as the territory of the *Southern Residents* (SR). The scientists are worried. At that time Springer is really still dependent on her mother's milk. She is not healthy and undernourished. Also the young female tends to get dangerously close to various boats, the large ferries in particular. On June 13, 2002 Springer is captured by the NMFS (US National Marine Fisheries Service) for her own good and brought to an enclosure. Veterinarians examine the whale. To avoid the young whale becoming too used to humans, living salmon are thrown into the enclosure. Beforehand the feed fish are injected with antibiotics to cure Springer. Exactly one

139

month after capture, on July 13, 2002, Springer is loaded onto a boat and brought 650 km to the north into the Johnstone Strait, the territory of the *Northern Residents* (NR). Initially she stays in a bay on Hanson Island, cordoned off from the sea with a net. When she is set free she first shoots off, then hesitates and plays in a forest of seaweed. During the following months she attaches herself to various groups of the A-pod, to which her family also belongs. For a while she roams around with her grandmother's (A24) group. Two whales show a conspicuous behaviour and keep pushing Springer away from the boats. The scientists register a special call, which they had so far only heard from Sutlej – high/deep(/high – "eoe". At the beginning of 2009 Springer is healthy and living with her relatives.

*8

1993: an unknown person shoots at A10 and her youngest calf (A47) from his boat. The mother takes the injured young to one of the approaching whale-watch boats. Both whales die during the following winter.

*9

1976: Six transient orcas are captured between Vancouver Island and the American mainland. Two of the animals are equipped with transmitter collars. The boxes are attached to the front edge of their fins with five thick screws each. To ensure that the transmitters drop away at some stage, the screw-nuts consist of a material, which decomposes after a few months. For ten days the scientists receive regular signals. For another five months they receive data sporadically. The whales survive, but they are left with terrible scars, as the screws remain in their fins even after the boxes have dropped away.

140

*10
Robson Bight – the Rubbing Beach
On August 20, 2007 a freight ship capsized and lost its cargo off Robson Bight, an area in the middle of the nature reserve between the north of Vancouver Island and the Canadian mainland. Amongst other things a tanker truck with over 10,000 litres of diesel. Since then the cargo had been lying at the bottom of the sea at a depth of 350 metres. Immediately after the accident great areas of the water surface were covered by fuel, but it was possible to avoid an absolute catastrophe. The disaster was recorded with underwater microphones: http://www.orcalab.org/news-archive/orcalab_general/07-08-21.html Only on May 12, 2009 the large-scale campaign for lifting the cargo was started. On May 15 the first barrels and objects were recovered. On May 19, after initial problems, the truck was finally recovered from the deep and hoisted onto the freight ship. A small amount of fuel (199 litres) leaked, but was removed immediately thanks to various precautionary measures taken by the recovery team.

Sources:

Alexandra Morton, "Die Sinfonie der Wale" (Listening to Whales), Malik
Ford, Ellis, Balcomb, Killer Whales, UBC Press
Ford, Ellis, Transients, UBC Press
Anthony Martin, Wale & Delphine, Mosaik Verlag
Carwardine, Hoyt, Fordyce, Gill, Wale, Delphine & Tümmler, Könemann
Erich Hoyt, ORCA – The Whale Called Killer, Camden House Publishing
Erich Hoyt, The Performing Orca – Why The Show Must Stop, WDCS
Kreutzkamp, Breiter, Westkanada Alaska, NaturReiseführer
Petra Deimer, Das Buch der Wale, Heyne
Verschiedene Autoren, Fische, Enzyklopädie der Tierwelt, Orbis
Verschiedene Autoren, Wale und Delphine, Jahr-Verlag GmbH

photo: Leona Niedzwiedz

Organisations

www.whales.org

delphinschutz.org/grd-english/index.html

www.greenpeace.org

Information about whales:

Homepage of Dr. Paul Spong and his wife Helena Symonds, who research the calls of the orcas on Hanson Island/Canada.
www.orcalab.org

Seasonal live transmission of the calls and up-to-date information about orca sightings.

www.orca-live.net

Orca calls for replaying and detailed information at www.orcinusorca.nl

www.whalemuseum.de

(German only) www.Pottwale.de

Symbolic adoption of Springer ("Lesja"):

http://www.bornfree.org.uk/give/adopt-an-animal/springer/

The contribution will be almost exclusively for the benefit of Paul Spong's Orcalab.

The authoress and the publishers are not responsible for the contents of the mentioned homepages.

Dr. Paul Spong, 2017:
"Since we wrote this (foreword), Springer has had two babies, and
is now the matriarch of her matriline, which is now assured to
continue into the future!"

"An unusual blessing for Doris Thomas:
May God always grant you the vision of an eagle,
the unbridled zest for life of a dolphin,
the patience of the divine spirit
and good persons,
who will always come to your assistance,
when you need their help and who will catch you,
when you fall.
God bless you!"

Father Markus Maiwald/Meitingen

146

Previously Published Children's Books

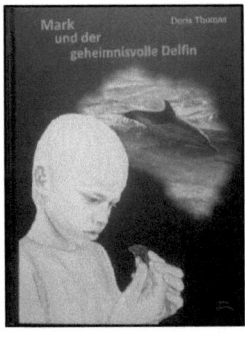

E-Book/Kindle too

www.Doris-T.de

English

Available on: Verlag an der ESTE (www.verlageste.de)

Motives for shirts, posters, artprint, pillows ...
on Redbubble and Spreadshirt